Welcome to Springwater, Montana. . . .

In full command of the storytelling magic that has made her a beloved, best-selling author, Linda Lael Miller spins her triumphant Western novel *Springwater* into a charming new series.

SPRINGWATER SEASONS is a breathtaking slice-of-life in a frontier town that's growing from little more than a whistle stop into a bustling Montana community. You will never forget the men and women who fall in love in these splendid tales, and you'll thrill along with them as Springwater blossoms with friendship, love, and laughter.

Don't miss a moment of life in Springwater—be sure to read these magnificent novels, each one a thrilling piece in the patchwork quilt that is

Springwater Seasons

Rachel
January 1999

Savannah
February 1999

Miranda
March 1999

Jessica
April 1999

Praise for Linda Lael Miller's Irresistible Western Romance

The Vow

"The Wild West comes alive through the loving touch of Linda Lael Miller's gifted words. . . . Breathtaking. . . . A romantic masterpiece. This one is a keeper you'll want to take down and read again and again."

—*Rendezvous*

"*The Vow* is a beautiful tale of love lost and regained. . . . The talented Linda Lael Miller provides a magical Western romance . . . that would be a masterpiece in any era."

—Amazon.com

"Linda Lael Miller's belief that we can have new starts is evident in *The Vow*. Everyone with the courage to try has a second chance to mend fences, reclaim dreams, uncover the past and move into a bright new future. Thus, *The Vow* is a romance that inspires us not only to rekindle passion, but to reclaim the love between a child and parent and to never be afraid to challenge ourselves to change for the better. Brava, Ms. Miller!"

—*Romantic Times*

"A beautiful tale. . . . *The Vow* is a heartwarming love story that is a combination of smoldering passion and sweet romance that uplifts readers to new heights. . . . FIVE STARS."

—*Affaire de Coeur*

Praise for

My Outlaw

"Ms. Miller's time travel novels are always precious but this one surpasses them all. The premise is incredibly invigorating, the passion hot and spicy. Memorable characters link it all together to create a keeper."

—*Rendezvous*

"Miller's reasoning is brilliant and will fascinate time-travel aficionados. . . . This sexy, smart, heart-stirring love story fulfills romance readers' dreams. This is destined to be a favorite."

—*Romantic Times*

"In one thousand years, a panel of twentieth-century experts discussing time travel novels will first talk about the works of H. G. Wells and Linda Lael Miller. [This] time travel romance has everything a reader could want in a novel. The story line is exciting and action-packed, with an incredible heroine who will do anything to save her beloved's life. *My Outlaw* is a keeper that will stand the test of time. . . . FIVE STARS."

—*Affaire de Coeur*

"Exhilarating. . . . Linda Lael Miller still reigns supreme in the time travel romance universe."

—Amazon.com

Also by Linda Lael Miller

Banner O'Brien
Corbin's Fancy
Memory's Embrace
My Darling Melissa
Angelfire
Desire and Destiny
Fletcher's Woman
Lauralee
Moonfire
Wanton Angel
Willow
Princess Annie
The Legacy
Taming Charlotte
Yankee Wife
Daniel's Bride
Lily and the Major
Emma and the Outlaw
Caroline and the Raider
Pirates
Knights
My Outlaw
The Vow
Two Brothers
Springwater

Springwater Seasons
Rachel
Savannah

Linda Lael Miller

SPRINGWATER SEASONS

Savannah

SONNET BOOKS

New York London Toronto Sydney Tokyo Singapore

This book is a work of fiction. Names, characters, places and
incidents are products of the author's imagination or are used
fictitiously. Any resemblance to actual events or locales or persons,
living or dead, is entirely coincidental.

An *Original* Publication of POCKET BOOKS

A Sonnet Book published by
POCKET BOOKS, a division of Simon & Schuster Inc.
1230 Avenue of the Americas, New York, NY 10020

Copyright © 1999 by Linda Lael Miller

ISBN: 0-671-02685-2

First Sonnet Books printing February 1999

10   9   8   7   6   5   4   3

SONNET BOOKS and colophon are trademarks of
Simon & Schuster Inc.

Cover art by Robert Hunt

Printed in the U.S.A.

June of 1998
Port Orchard

Dear Friends,

Welcome to the Springwater stagecoach station, which will grow over the next few months, before your very eyes, into a thriving community, complete with a saloon, a schoolhouse, a church, and a newspaper, among other things. There are six books in the Springwater series, although I may do more. I love the idea of writing a long, involved story and watching this fictional town full of delightful people come to life. I hope the many and varied characters will become as dear to you as they are to me.

Let me know what you think, and to receive a copy of the *Springwater Gazette,* Springwater's own newspaper, please send a business-sized stamped, self-addressed envelope, with your address clearly printed. We'll add you to the newsletter list automatically, thus giving you advance notice of every new release, whether it is part of this series or not. The address is:

Linda Lael Miller
P.O. Box 669
Port Orchard, WA 98366
e-mail: lindalaelm@aol.com

God bless and keep.

Warmly,

Linda Lael Miller

For Kate Collins,
always gentle, always sweet, always *there.*
Thanks.

Savannah

CHAPTER

1

Summer, 1875

THE GIRL MOANING on the opposite stagecoach seat
was painfully young, by Savannah's astute reckoning,
not more than seventeen. She was probably very pretty
under normal circumstances, with her thick chestnut-
colored hair and wide-set violet eyes, but for now, with
her belly swollen nearly to the bursting point under the
front of that tattered calico dress, and her face con-
torted in an agonizing effort not to scream, she just
looked small and scared and very much alone.

Savannah nudged the dark-haired, beard-stubbled
man slouched on the seat beside her, gazing out the
window as if he were trying to will himself away to
someplace far from the interior of that smotheringly
hot, cramped, and bouncing stagecoach. He wasn't
much past thirty, but he might have been Methuselah's
older brother if you went by the look in his eyes. "Do
something," she commanded, in an impatient whisper.
She knew he was a doctor of some sort, for all that he'd
spent most of his time in the smokier recesses of the

Hell-bent Saloon, having turned up in Choteau a week or so before. He'd promptly lost his horse in a faro game, and Savannah had taken it as a bad omen when he'd suddenly boarded that same stage. She'd planned on having it to herself, at least as far as Springwater station.

He smelled of whiskey, old cigar smoke, and a soul-deep sorrow, his dark hair was rumpled, and he was sorely in need of a shave, as well as clean clothes, a decent meal or two, and a good night's sleep. He'd taken the seat across from Savannah and kept his thoughts to himself, at least until the driver had stopped the rig somewhere along the trail—quite literally in the middle of nowhere—to pick up the pregnant girl. He'd moved to Savannah's side then, with a desultory sort of courtesy, to make room for the newcomer.

Savannah nudged him again, for she was used to having her orders obeyed, and promptly. "Did you hear me?" she whispered, though there was, of course, no hope that the girl wouldn't hear as well, jammed in knee-to-knee with her fellow passengers the way she was. "This child needs your help!"

"I'm not that kind of doctor," he ground out, with a long breath. He carried a time-beaten medical bag at his feet, his only visible baggage, a flag of his profession, though his clothes were sorry indeed—scuffed boots, Army issue no doubt, dark trousers worn to a shine, a once-white shirt of good linen, and black leather suspenders. He had especially fine teeth, Savannah noticed, for the first time, and, under all that self-absorption and debauchery, his features were aristocratic ones, finely carved. His jawline was strong and square, his mouth sensual and expressive.

"I don't care if you're a *horse* doctor," Savannah snapped back, ready to elbow him again, and with a lot more force, if necessary. In fact, she was quite prepared to open her beaded drawstring bag and ferret out her derringer, should matters come to such a pass, and insist that he do his duty as a physician. "Either you look after this girl or you'll have me to deal with."

"She's going to have a baby," he answered, as though this clever diagnosis should suffice to settle the entire matter once and for all.

Savannah might have struck him with her derringer-weighted bag, if there hadn't been such a dire need for him to remain conscious. "Jupiter and Zeus," she swore, "any fool could see that!" She paused, trying for a semblance of diplomacy. "She needs some help getting it done, Doc. And we're all she's got at the moment. You and me."

The girl sank her teeth into her lower lip, gasping and clutching her protruding stomach with a pair of grubby hands. She looked as though she'd just come from weeding some vegetable patch or mucking out a pigpen, and she didn't smell a whole lot better.

The doctor sighed and sat forward. "What's your name?" he asked, with a sort of gruff gentleness that raised Savannah's opinion of him, though only a little, and briefly.

"Mir-Miranda," she said. "Miranda Leebrook."

He reached down for his bag, lifted it onto his lap, and rummaged inside. Taking out a bottle and a bit of surprisingly pristine cloth, he doused his hands with a pungent chemical of some sort, and wiped them clean. "Where did you come from? I understood there weren't many homesteads out this far."

It seemed to Savannah that Miranda attempted a smile, though it might have been a grimace of pain. "My pa and me had words, and he put me out to make my own way. We was headed toward Butte in the wagon, me and Lorelei and him."

"What about the father of this baby?" the doctor asked crisply, but without judgment or rancor. "Where's he?"

Tears glistened in Miranda's expressive pansy-purple eyes. "He's a long time gone," she said. "Won't never be back, neither."

Savannah's heart constricted at this, but she was used to hearing stories, all sorts of stories, and she'd learned a long time ago that it didn't pay to go wading too deep into other folks' troubles. She said nothing, but simply pounded hard on the roof of the coach with the handle of her parasol.

The driver brought the coach to a bone-jostling stop, while the conversation between doctor and patient continued, quiet and calm on his part, breathless on hers, and interwoven with frantic cries.

A broad, dusty face, rimmed in an aura of ginger hair, appeared at the window opening. "There a problem back here, ma'am?" the young driver asked.

Savannah held her temper. "Yes," she said, putting a

fine point on the word nonetheless, and aiming for a soft spot. "One of us seems to be giving birth. The doctor here is prepared to deliver the child, but it would certainly help if the coach weren't rolling and pitching the whole time."

The driver looked regretful, and tugged at the brim of his disreputable hat. "We ain't but three miles from the station, ma'am. It's just the other side of Willow Creek." He glanced in a westerly direction, tracking the sun. "We got to keep goin'. It'll be dark soon, and that's no time for decent folks to be out and about."

Savannah was beyond exasperation. "Can't you see that this girl—?"

The young man shook his head and settled his hat again. "I'm sorry, ma'am. Miss June-bug McCaffrey, up ahead at Springwater, she'll take good care of the whole matter. We got to press on." With that, he was gone, the coach bouncing on its springs as he climbed back into the box to take up the reins again.

The doctor was already engaged in a thorough if awkward examination of his patient. Savannah looked away quickly, but not quickly enough to spare herself a burning flush of embarrassment. For all her reputation, she was not a loose woman, and she had the appropriate sensibilities.

"Can't you say something to the driver?" Savannah demanded. She had little to contribute at the moment, but for her opinions, which seemed unwelcome.

The physician shrugged one sturdy shoulder. "Sounds to me like he's got his mind made up," he said, and gently covered Miranda's legs with her skirts again.

He got out the chemical and another cloth and began to wash his hands once more. "Besides, I think you've said enough for all of us."

"Is my baby going to be all right?" Miranda asked, in a tiny voice.

He pulled the stethoscope from around his neck and tossed it back into the ancient bag. Then he flashed a smile, so unexpectedly, ferociously charming that Savannah was taken aback, though for just the merest moment. "I'd wager a good deal that that child is just fine," he said. "Eight pounds, maybe ten, with the constitution of a mule."

Savannah recalled the perfectly good horse this man had lost at faro and refrained, for Miranda's sake, from pointing out that wagering was clearly not his greatest talent. The stagecoach lurched forward again, pitching and rolling over the rocky ground, nearly sending both Savannah and the doctor hurtling across the small gap between seats onto the girl.

"Can we make it as far as the stagecoach station?" Savannah hissed, though there was, of course, no hope that Miranda hadn't heard.

He raised one dark eyebrow. "We can," he said, "but there might be four of us by the time we arrive."

Panic roared into Savannah like floodwaters into a gulch, swirling and splashing and tearing things up by their roots. In her eventful lifetime, she'd helped her father, a barber and erstwhile undertaker in Kansas City, Missouri, to remove everything from common splinters to bullets, arrows, and buckshot from human flesh, and her grandmother had been a midwife of sorts, full of tales and legends. For all that, the idea of actually *witnessing* childbirth made her light-headed.

She swayed slightly, and pressed the fingertips of her right hand to one temple.

The doctor's face darkened. "I'm fresh out of smelling salts," he told her, in a sharp whisper. "So don't you go falling apart on me."

Savannah was incensed at the suggestion, even though there had been some merit to it. She stiffened her spine and shot him a look fit to pierce a dartboard. "I am quite all right, thank you," she said.

Miranda, perspiring profusely now, began to whimper. "It hurts," she said. "It hurts real bad."

He shoved a hand through his mussed hair. "Yep," he said, resigned. "I imagine it does."

Savannah was once again seized by the desire to strike the man with something heavy; instead, she moved over to sit beside Miranda, draping one arm around the poor little creature's thin and quivering shoulders. "We'll be at the stagecoach station soon," she said, and though she was speaking gently for the young woman's sake, she was gazing at the doctor, and she knew her eyes were snapping with fury. "There'll be a nice clean bed for you to lie down in. Everything will be all right, you'll see."

"Where were you headed, anyway?" asked the doctor, ignoring Savannah's displeasure to watch Miranda's face with narrowed eyes.

"No place in particular," Miranda gasped out, her

back arching, seemingly of its own volition. "I reckon me and the babe would've died out there, if it weren't for this stage coming along just when it did."

Savannah spared a bitter thought or two for Miranda's uncaring father, but the present situation was far too desperate to allow for much distraction.

"What about your mother?" the doctor pressed. "Didn't she try to intercede for you?"

"I don't guess I know what that means," Miranda confessed, pressing each word, separate and distinct, between tightly clenched teeth. "For somebody to 'intercede,' I mean. Anyway, my ma's been dead a long while now. The woman my pa took up with—her name's Lorelei—doesn't have much use for me."

"Take it easy," he said, giving the young woman both his hands, which she squeezed fiercely against the pain. "Breathe slowly and deeply. We're going to look after you, Miss—er—well, this lady and I."

"It would comfort me some to know your right names," Miranda said.

"I'm Savannah Rigbey," Savannah responded gently, wishing there were something, anything, she could do to ease the girl's suffering.

"Parrish," the doctor added, and though his tone was cordial enough, the glance he spared Savannah was a mite on the grudging side. "Prescott Parrish."

The coach hurtled downhill, careening wildly from side to side, fit to fling open both doors and toss them out; and then it splashed into axle-deep water. Savannah peered out at Willow Creek with alarm, half-blinded by the late-day light dancing on the water. She might have prayed then, if she hadn't given up on God a long time before. It wasn't deep, that stream, but she had a swift and terrifying vision of the coach turning over, trapping all of them inside.

"We're almost there," Dr. Parrish said, while the girl continued to grip his hands.

Miranda flung back her head and shrieked like a mountain cat. Her teeth were bared and she writhed, as leanly muscular as any lioness. When she got her breath, she cried out to God for help and mercy, and Savannah and the doctor exchanged yet another look, not heated this time, but somber.

The team scrambled up the opposite bank of the creek, dragging the half-rolling, half-floating coach behind. The ride was so rough after that that Savannah half-expected the baby to shake loose of Miranda's insides and bounce right out onto the narrow floor.

The mother-to-be alternated between screaming her lungs out and making a pitiful, keening sound, something like a long, unbroken sob. Her colorless dress was nearly wet through now, though when Savannah gave Parrish a questioning glance, he shook his head.

"Water hasn't broken," he said.

Savannah hoped that was a good sign, but she didn't think so. She recognized the quiet worry in Prescott Parrish's dark eyes, even if Miranda couldn't.

At last, at last, the driver shouted something to the horses, a coarse and unintelligible roar, and the brakes screeched against the iron-rimmed wheels, grinding the coach to a halt in a great surging billow of gritty, yellow-brown dust.

"Springwaaaater staaation!" he called out, as though there might be some confusion on the part of his passengers.

Dr. Parrish thrust the door open and jumped down, pulling Miranda off the seat and into his arms. "Bring the bag!" he commanded, and Savannah complied, hurrying after him through the roiling dust.

A tall man with very dark hair and kindly eyes awaited them on the porch of the station house, arms folded. "Best get her bedded down right quick," he said. "Straight through the dining room, at the far end of the hall."

Parrish nodded and strode on, and Savannah followed, coughing from the dust. Springwater station was her final destination, for the moment, since Trey Hargreaves and his new wife were already occupying the space over the Brimstone Saloon. She would rent a room and stay on here until she and her business partner could work out some other arrangement.

"Jacob McCaffrey," said the tall man when she was inside. He offered a large, work-gnarled hand in greeting.

"Savannah Rigbey," she responded, watching out of the corner of her eye as Parrish disappeared down the indicated hallway. "I understand your wife might be able to assist the doctor—"

McCaffrey shook his head. "She's on the mountain, my June-bug, tendin' to Granny Johnson. The old lady's laid up with rheumatiz."

Savannah felt her knees go weak. "Isn't there someone—?"

"Miss Rigbey!" Parrish bellowed, from somewhere in the back of the station. "Kindly get your bustle in here!"

She looked desperately up at Mr. McCaffrey, but he merely shrugged.

"Jupiter and Zeus," Savannah muttered, unpinning her hat and setting it aside, then shaking the dust from her skirts as best she could. "I'm coming!" she called back and, after straightening her spine and squaring her shoulders, she marched toward the distinctly unsettling sounds of childbirth, bringing the doctor's bag along with her.

Parrish had laid the girl on the pristine sheets of a wide bed, and was shoving up his sleeves as Savannah entered the room. He didn't spare her so much as a glance. "Get me hot water, and all the clean cloth you can find," he commanded, his voice a brusque bark.

Had things been different, Savannah would have told him what to do with his orders, but this was the exception. Whatever her private views might be regarding Parrish, he *was* a doctor, and therefore badly needed at the moment. She set the bag down within his easy reach and hurried out to obey.

The baby, a strapping boy with bunched fists and pumping feet, was delivered less than half an hour later. Parrish cut the cord competently, washed and bundled the infant, and handed him to his breathless, beaming mother.

"He's right handsome, isn't he?" she said.

Savannah, still struck by the messy splendor of the experience, couldn't help wondering what would become of the two of them, Miranda and her brand-new baby, alone in a remote place like this, with no money and no prospects. She blinked back uncharacteristic tears and averted her eyes.

"I told you he'd be big as a mule," said the doctor, scrubbing his hands at the basin by then. He nodded to Savannah, indicating that he wanted the linens changed on Miranda's bed, and she proceeded to comply, skillfully managing the task without disturbing mother and baby overmuch.

He went out then, without another word, and Savannah supposed he'd board the next stagecoach, come the morning, and move on to wherever he'd been headed in the first place. She certainly wouldn't miss him, but she was grateful that he'd delivered Miranda's baby, however unwillingly, and she wished him well.

When both Miranda and the baby were sleeping comfortably, Savannah left the room and asked to be directed to her own chamber, which turned out to be a small nook behind the kitchen stove. Two buckets of hot water awaited her there, along with her few bags, and she undressed behind a scarred folding screen and washed herself from head to foot, then put on fresh clothes, a blue bombazine skirt and white shirtwaist, deceptively prim. Gazing into the small, cracked mirror affixed to the inside wall, she arranged her mass of red-gold hair in a neat cloud around her face, and pinched some color into her wan cheeks. For all her effort, her light blue eyes revealed her weariness, and a lot more besides.

She made herself leave the tiny room and join Mr.

McCaffrey and Dr. Parrish at the table nearest the fireplace. They were drinking coffee and talking in low tones, but when Savannah appeared, they both stood, McCaffrey readily, with the easy, practiced grace of a gentleman, Parrish causing the bench legs to scrape against the floor as he thrust himself to his feet, a moment too late for good manners.

"Evenin'," Jacob McCaffrey said. Only then did she notice the fair-haired boy and the beautiful Indian girl playing checkers on the hearth nearby. Both of them looked up at her in mild speculation.

"Good evening," Savannah said. She played at being a lady whenever she could, but it was a facade, with no substance behind it, and she suspected everyone else in the room knew that as well as she did, even the children. She'd stepped off the narrow path—or, more properly, been dragged off—a long time before.

"Toby," McCaffrey said, in his rumbling, summer-thunder voice, "fetch Miss Rigbey some of them dumplin's and a little chicken. I reckon she's hungry by now."

Savannah hadn't eaten since the night before, having left Choteau very early that morning, well before the woman at the rooming house where she'd stayed since her arrival in the territory was willing to serve breakfast, but she found she had no appetite. She shook her head. "I'll just brew a pot of tea, if that's all right."

The Indian girl scrambled to her feet. "I'll do that for you," she said, with cheerful resolution. "You must be my pa's partner."

Savannah smiled, finally realizing that this was Trey's

daughter, the child he had spoken of so often during their long association. "Yes," she said. "And you're Emma!"

Emma nodded. "I don't think he's expecting you," she said. "He got himself married a while back, you know. A year ago last spring."

"I had word that he meant to take a wife," Savannah said, well aware that Parrish and the stationmaster, and probably the boy, too, were watching her with new interest. "I hope they'll be very happy together."

Emma was intent on ladling water into a big kettle with a spout and setting it on to boil. With the easy skill of a grown woman, she built up the fire and adjusted the damper. "They're happy, all right," she said. "Pa's going to build us a big house, the kind you send off for. The boards and windows and things are supposed to get here any day now. Then we'll all live together, me and Pa and Rachel, like a real family." Her smile broadened. "We got us a mortgage!"

Savannah laid a hand on the girl's shoulder and smiled gently. "You must miss living with your father," she said.

Emma looked up at her with shining eyes. "I don't mind staying here. Me and Toby, we play checkers most all the time, and do our schoolwork together. Besides, I see my pa every day, and Rachel's our teacher—she's my stepmother, but I have to call her 'Mrs. Hargreaves' at school—so I don't get lonesome for her, either." She lowered her voice confidentially. "Except sometimes late at night, when I can't get to sleep."

The men had gone back to their quiet talk, making Savannah feel less self-conscious. "I'm sure it won't be long," she said to Emma, "until you're all together again in your big new house."

Emma's brow crumpled with concern. "That lady in there was screaming a lot, while she was having her baby. It must have hurt something powerful."

Savannah saw no point in lying. "That's so," she admitted. "But it's over now, and she's got the child to show for her pains." For all the good that would do a scrap of a girl, alone and penniless in the wilds of Montana Territory, she added to herself.

"Miss Rachel—I think she's going to have a baby, too," Emma said, in that same confidential undertone. "I don't reckon me or my pa could stand seeing her hurt like that, though."

Savannah gave the child a gentle squeeze around the shoulders. "Don't you fret," she said. "It's a natural thing. Your stepmother will be just fine, and so will the rest of you." She couldn't imagine what made her speak with such authority, given her utter lack of experience with such matters, except that she liked Trey's daughter and didn't want her to worry.

"You'd better have yourself some of these chicken and dumplings," Emma said wisely, lifting the lid of a cast-iron pot and peering inside. "Jacob made them, but they aren't halfways bad."

Savannah laughed, more relaxed than before. "Maybe I'm a little hungry after all," she admitted, and soon she was seated at one of the tables, far from the men, consuming a plateful of food. When she'd washed her dish and utensils and put them away, she went in to check on Miranda and the baby.

The girl was awake, admiring her little son, and her eyes shone with a queer mingling of pride and sorrow when she looked at Savannah. "He's the image of his daddy, Jack Worgan."

Savannah drew a deep breath and let it out slowly, searching for words. In her line of work, she'd heard just about every story there was, and she figured that Worgan was either dead, married, or just plain gone. She had a personal rule against prying, so all she said was "That's nice."

Tears pooled along Miranda's lower lashes. "I don't have the first idea what we're going to do, my baby and me. I been asking God for help right along, but there sure hasn't been any clap of thunder nor burning bush."

Had she been a religious woman, which she wasn't, Savannah might have pointed out that some folks would construe the stagecoach's coming along when it had as an answer to prayer. The same might have been said of Dr. Parrish's help, too, slow as he'd been to give it, and of the waiting shelter and safety of Springwater station. "We'll think of something," she said, and it was bravado, pure and simple, for Savannah knew full well just how limited a woman's choices really were.

There was teaching, and even if that appointment hadn't been held by Trey's wife, Rachel, Miranda clearly wasn't qualified. There was marriage—prospects seemed a bit scant, Springwater being smack in the middle of the wilderness—or household service, which wasn't so different from being a wife, except that a body could expect to be paid for her drudgery. No grand houses around, either, in need of servants. The last choice was whoring, in all its many forms. That was how most people saw Savannah's way of earning a living, as a form of prostitution, even though she'd never in her life slept with a man for money.

"I can work hard as any man," Miranda said anxiously. "If somebody'll just give me half the chance——"

Savannah looked away. She could have offered the girl a job of work herself, entertaining the men at the Brimstone Saloon—but of course *that* would be no favor. And what would become of the child, growing up in such a place? She forced herself to meet Miranda's gaze again. "Let me make a crib for that baby of yours," she said. Then she removed a drawer from the bureau, set it carefully across the seats of two straight-backed chairs, and padded the inside with a blanket. That done, she gently took the sleeping infant from Miranda's arms and laid him down in the improvised cradle. "What are you going to call him?" she asked, hoping, for a reason she couldn't explain, that it wouldn't be "Jack," after his absent father.

"I want to give him a good, solid, Bible name," Miranda said, settling into the fluffy feather mattress with a yawn. "Isaiah, maybe. Or Ezekiel."

Savannah smiled. "Shall I bring you a plate? Mr. McCaffrey made chicken and dumplings."

Miranda shook her head and yawned again. "No, thanks, ma'am," she said. "More than anything, I want to sleep a spell."

"A good idea," Savannah agreed gently, and started toward the door.

"Wait," Miranda said quickly, and with a note of soft urgency in her voice.

Savannah stopped. The room was filled with twilight now; soon, it would be pitch dark. She expected the girl to ask for a lantern.

"I'm grateful," Miranda said. "To you and to the doc and to that stagecoach driver, too. I guess me and little Isaiah or Ezekiel would be in a grievous plight by now, if it weren't for you folks."

Savannah merely nodded, not trusting herself to speak, and slipped out, closing the door softly behind her.

"You look mighty sorrowful," Mr. McCaffrey remarked, when she turned to find him leaning against the mantel of the big fireplace, drawing on a pipe. There was no sign of the children or, for that matter, of Dr. Parrish. No doubt he'd already struck out for the Brimstone Saloon, there to spend whatever money he might have left on liquor and games of chance.

"I'm worried about Miranda," she admitted, though not until she was well away from the doorway leading to the hall, lest the girl should overhear. "She's got no folks to look after her, no man either."

"I kinda figured that," McCaffrey remarked. "I've got an idea my June-bug will be able to come up with a solution or two, though. She has a way of makin' places for lost sheep. You may have noticed we've got a stray or two around here already."

Savannah sagged onto one of the benches and rested

her elbows on the tabletop, propping her chin in her palms. "Emma and the boy—Toby?"

"I wouldn't consider Emma a stray, exactly. Her papa loves her somethin' fierce. But Toby, now, he was alone in the world, for all practical intents and purposes, until we took him in. And then there's Christabel— she's with June-bug, lookin' after Granny. She's got one lame foot, Christabel has, and a heart that's bigger than she is. Anyhow, I don't imagine Miss Miranda and her baby will be that much more trouble."

"You mean, you'll just let them stay here, indefinitely?"

"I don't see what else we can do. Wouldn't be right nor proper to turn them out, after all."

Savannah dashed at her eyes with the back of one hand, much heartened by the man's kindness. She hadn't seen much of that kind of charity in her own travels, had almost given up hope that it existed. "Thank you, Mr. McCaffrey," she said, with a sniffle. She was just tired, she reasoned to herself, that was all. She'd long since corralled and tamed all her emotions—it was safer not to care too much about anything or anyone.

"Jacob," he corrected her, with the slightest shadow of a smile. She hadn't known him long, but it was clear that when Jacob smiled, it was an occasion in itself.

She put out her hand, as though they were meeting for the first time. "Savannah, then," she insisted, and sniffled again.

He set the pipe on the mantel and came to sit down across the table from her. "You don't look much like a saloon-keepin' woman," he observed. "More like a schoolmarm, or the lady of a big, fancy house."

Coming from anyone else, the remark might have stung, but Savannah knew Jacob was merely curious. Although she suspected he could be stern when the situation called for it, his was a benign and gentle spirit. She heaved a sigh. "My story is a long one, Jacob, and it's complicated. I'm not sure I'm ready to tell it just yet."

"That's fine," Jacob answered easily. The station door opened just then, spilling a shadowy chill across the smooth plank floor. "We all got our secrets."

Dr. Parrish came in, looking sober if no neater than before. He pushed the door closed behind him. What secrets, Savannah wondered, what scandals and sorrows, had made him what he was?

CHAPTER

2

THE FLICKERING LIGHT of the evening fire made
Savannah Rigbey look more like a ministering angel
than what Pres knew her to be—a saloon-keeper and
quite possibly something a whole lot less respectable.
She'd handled herself admirably well during the deliv-
ery earlier—it had been untidy work, though tame
compared with what he was used to—and he'd noticed
her pallor and the grimly determined set of her chin
and shoulders. Every time the girl, Miranda, had
screamed, she'd flinched, as though feeling an echo of
the pain in her own body.

Now, coming upon her unexpectedly, in the main
room of the stagecoach station, he thought she seemed
smaller than before, more fragile. And, somehow, lit
from within.

"Evenin'," said McCaffrey, sparing him a nod.

Pres thrust splayed fingers through his hair and then
inclined his head in response to the other man's sparse
greeting. He wasn't drunk, though the inside of his

head still felt scraped and hollow from the last bout of elbow-bending in Choteau, but all of the sudden he was aware of his seedy appearance in a way that had not troubled him for a very long time. He yearned for a bath, a shave, fresh clothes, and a place in polite company.

"Didn't see where you had any baggage to speak of, Doc," McCaffrey observed, while Savannah just sat there, at one of the long tables, watching Pres in silent speculation. "You just passin' through, or meaning to light right here at Springwater? Town's growin'. Folks have bought land for a newspaper office and a general store, and the Territorial Governor has promised to appoint a U.S. Marshal to keep the peace. We could use a doctor, too."

Pres had just come from the spring that gave the place its name; he'd gone for a walk after seeing to the girl and her baby, to stretch his legs and calm his nerves. As far as he was concerned, Springwater didn't qualify as a town, with just a stagecoach station, a schoolhouse and a saloon to call its own, but he saw no point in saying so. He broke the trance that had held him in place, just inside the doorway, and shook his head, proceeding toward the cookstove at the far end of the room.

"I'm moving on with the next stage," he said, taking an enamel mug from a shelf and filling it with strong black coffee from a pot on the back of the range. He'd know the place he was meant to wind up when he got to it and, once there, he expected to settle in and drink himself to death, swamped by his own demons. Matter of fact, he'd been slowly killing himself for a long time, and most days it seemed he was succeeding.

Turning around, mug in hand and raised halfway to his mouth, he caught Savannah looking at him, though her expression was unreadable in that light. She glanced away quickly, if not quickly enough. "I'm not the sort of doctor you need, anyway," he felt obliged to add. An odd thing in itself, that inclination to expand on the matter of his general insufficiency, as he'd long since decided that his life, his preferences, and his problems were nobody's business but his own.

McCaffrey arched a dark, bushy eyebrow. "We ain't real choosy, to tell you the truth," he said. "If you're better with horses than people, that's all right, too."

Pres laughed at that, and the response was so unpracticed, so unfamiliar, that it came out as a sort of rasp. This time, he saw a quick, glittering flash of annoyance in Savannah's eyes; it pleased him to know he'd nettled her, if only a little, though he wasn't sure why. "I am—or was—a surgeon," he said, drawn into the circle of firelight, almost against his will. He took a seat across the table from Savannah, while Jacob McCaffrey remained standing, one elbow raised and braced against the pinewood mantel.

Savannah spoke at last. "You 'were' a surgeon?" she asked; her voice was soft, but not pitying. "What happened?"

He saw it all again, the blood, the mangled limbs and scattered parts, heard the canon fire and the shrieks. Worst of all, he heard the pleas, for mercy, for death, for an end to the pain. The pleas he couldn't grant. Some of the coffee spilled over as he set the mug down. "The war," he ground out. "The war happened."

"We lost two sons at Chattanooga," McCaffrey said. "Will and Wesley were their names. Twins." He paused, and his voice seemed to come from long ago and far away. "They were good boys. Friend of ours saw them fall, one and then the other. They were born together, and they died together. I guess that's fittin', but it like to have broke their mother's heart, and I don't believe I'll ever put the grievin' entirely behind me, either." The big man sighed and then returned to himself. For him, Pres knew, the story constituted an oration. "I reckon they're buried in unmarked graves, but at least they're in Tennessee."

Savannah was watching McCaffrey with her heart in her face, and Pres was watching her. He couldn't seem to help it. She looked so different in her prim, schoolmarmish clothes, somehow even more alluring than in the bright, flouncing silks, satins, bangles, and feathers she'd worn to sing and peddle drinks at the Hell-bent Saloon, back in Choteau. He wondered what sort of past had brought her to such a present.

She was a soiled dove, a lady of the evening, Pres reminded himself, and he was a used-up, throw-away drunk, friendless, and literally down to his last nickel. What a sorry pair they made, misfits, both of them. Lost souls.

Again, he shoved a hand through his hair.

"I'd better show you where to bed down before you fall over," Jacob said. "You want any supper? Hot water, maybe?"

Pres couldn't have forced down so much as a bite of food, but the offer of clean water had a distinct appeal. "A bath wouldn't hurt me," he allowed, and caught Savannah with a look of devout agreement on her face. He almost laughed again, but he was too tired, too dispirited, too long out of practice, and his throat still hurt from the last time. For a moment, he wanted very much to stay in Springwater, to find himself again, to build a simple country practice, like the one his father had had, at home in Maine. He'd found a semblance of peace, standing by that spring and watching the first stars rise against the wide sky, had even thought he might be able to lay himself down and sleep through a whole night, here in this quiet place. A grand illusion, all of that, he'd reminded himself then, as he did now. It was the waking nightmares that were real, the screaming and incessant carnage, the black flies and the putrid stenches. He had to keep moving, stay a step ahead of the memories, lest they pull him under like quicksand.

"Come along, then," McCaffrey said, matter-of-factly. "I'll see to the water and find you some fresh clothes for tomorrow."

Pres finished his coffee, stood, and carried the cup over to the cast-iron sink, near the cookstove. That done, he followed the stationmaster to a small room at the back, hardly bigger than a closet, but blessedly clean, with the distant sound of the springs coming in through an open window. The bed was narrow, and covered in an ancient, neatly pieced quilt with a date— 1847—and a partial Bible verse embroidered in the center panel. *Seek ye first the kingdom of God* . . .

"I don't have the money to pay for this room," Pres said, moved to confession by the other man's quiet generosity, "or for the bathwater and soap, either. I've got five cents and a stagecoach ticket to my name and I need them both."

"I didn't figure you was real flush," Jacob replied, obviously a master of understatement. "We got water and soap aplenty, and the room's just settin' here, empty as the Lord's tomb, so you might as well be in it as out there in the barn or on the ground someplace. I'll fetch the tub while you're making yourself comfortable."

Comfortable. When had he last enjoyed that blissful state? At home in Rocky Cove, eating his mother's cooking, sleeping in the sheets she kept clean and crisply pressed, accompanying his father on rounds. It all seemed so distant and unreal that he might have been reflecting on the life of some long-dead stranger, rather than his own innocent youth.

Jacob McCaffrey had slipped out sometime during this revery, closing the door behind him. Pres went to the window, more because he couldn't stand still than because he thought there was anything to see. His hands shook even when he grasped the sill to steady them, and he felt a pinch in the pit of his stomach as he stared out on that moonless night. It was an excellent metaphor, all that dark nothingness, he thought, for the ruined and desolate landscape of his own soul.

He rubbed his beard-roughened jaw. It seemed a supreme irony, craving whiskey, for he truly despised the stuff, but crave it he did, especially in still and lonely moments like these. In spite of the way it branded the inside of his belly at every swallow like molten steel.

Without it, though, there wouldn't be the remotest chance of even closing his eyes, let alone sleeping. He had not, in fact, enjoyed a night of natural rest without the aid of whiskey or laudanum since before his enlistment in the Union Army, in the summer of 1862. He'd been full of ideals then, fresh out of medical college and damnably certain of his ability to save the world.

Mercifully, Jacob returned in the midst of these ruminations, forcing back some of the gloom by the simple but palpable force of his presence, carrying a sizable round washtub, lined with copper. After that, he began lugging in water, with the boy, Toby, helping him. Towels were provided, along with a bar of rough yellow soap, an extra bucket of water, a straight razor, and a leather strop. The promised change of clothes appeared, too—a loose, butternut-colored shirt, worn to a chamoislike smoothness, and a pair of rough-spun trousers, black like his own.

"Will's things, or Wesley's," Jacob said, by way of

explanation. "Miss June-bug looked for our boys to come back for a long while—I guess she hoped the reports were wrong—and kept a lot of their belongings lest they be needed."

Pres felt his throat tighten and go painfully dry. He might have seen the McCaffreys' sons in his travels, might even have treated one or the other, for he'd tended Union soldiers and rebels alike, during his term of service, scrambling from one battleground, one field hospital, one ambulance wagon to another. Never doing anybody a damn bit of good, no matter how hard he worked.

"Thanks," he ground out, and took the clothes. "Maybe I ought to look in on the girl and her baby once more."

"Miss Savannah's with them just now," Jacob countered easily. "You have your bath and get yourself some sleep. There'll be another stage through tomorrow afternoon sometime."

Pres nodded, and then McCaffrey and the boy were gone. He peeled away his clothes—couldn't rightly remember the last time he'd changed, let alone scrubbed himself down—and stepped gingerly into the tub full of water. It was cooling by then, but it still felt good.

He soaked awhile, then scoured, soaked, and scoured again. Finally, he stood up and poured the bucket of now-tepid water over his head, for good measure. The floor was awash when he stepped out and reached for the towel; he dried himself and wrapped the bit of cloth around his middle. Except for the glow of the kerosene lamp burning on the bedside table, the room was black.

He wouldn't sleep, of course, with no whiskey to numb the edges of his mind, and he still wasn't hungry, but he did feel a little better all the same. Downright inspired, he sharpened the razor against the strop, lathered his jaw with soap suds, and shaved. Time he got done, he was out-and-out handsome, in a rascally sort of way.

The bed looked inviting, all of the sudden. He tossed aside the towel, put out the lamp, threw back the covers, and lay down, just to feel the clean sheets against his bare skin. The next thing he knew, sunlight was drumming crimson at his eyelids.

The homey sounds of clattering stove-lids and a woman's voice, singing softly, awoke Savannah on that first morning at Springwater; for the briefest of moments, she thought she was back home in Kansas City, before her long fall from grace, that it was her grandmother on the other side of that wall, working her way through a vast repertoire of hymns and spirituals while she made breakfast. Then, of course, she remembered that she was far from that time and place, and blinked rapidly a couple of times before she got a hold on her emotions. Then she rose, put on her skirt and shirtwaist from the night before, along with a pair of soft kid slippers, and went out to face the day.

A pretty woman with silver-streaked brown hair and bright blue eyes was standing before the stove, spatula in hand, and her smile washed over Savannah like a spill of bright sunlight. "Mornin'," she said. "You must be Trey's friend Savannah."

Savannah nodded, knowing without being told that this was June-bug McCaffrey, back from her mission of mercy to Granny Johnson's place up in the foothills. June-bug told her who she was anyway, and Savannah was charmed; it was easy to see why the stationmistress was one of Trey's favorite people. There was a gentle competence about her, an innate grace, that warmed and welcomed.

Mrs. McCaffrey laughed. "Set yourself down and I'll pour you some coffee. Whew, but I had to hit the floor a-runnin' this mornin', we've got us such a houseful, 'tween the kids and the doc and that poor girl in there with her baby!" She seemed pleased to be cooking for a crowd, for her eyes were shining and her lovely skin was flushed with exuberant color.

"How is Miranda? Has the doctor been to see her yet?"

"Doc's still sleepin', far as I know," June-bug confided, flipping half a dozen flapjacks in rapid sequence with a skillful motion of her wrist. "Miranda's just fine, though. She's already had some breakfast and her milk's in, too, so little Isaiah-or-Ezekiel is right contented. You set down, now. I don't want to have to tell you again."

Well aware that she would lose any argument, Savannah sat down, and allowed June-bug to serve her coffee and then a plateful of pancakes swimming in brown-sugar molasses and fresh butter. She ate with her usual good appetite, and was just finishing up when Dr. Parrish appeared, looking clean and rested and therefore quite unlike his former self. He'd even shaved, and his clothes were a great improvement over the garments he'd been wearing the day before.

He looked faintly surprised to Savannah, as though he'd expected to wake up somewhere else, or not to wake up at all. Like her, she deduced, in a flash of insight, he was used to being an outsider, never quite fitting in anywhere.

"Morning," he said, somewhat sheepishly, nodding to Savannah and then to June-bug. "I'm obliged for the use of these clothes."

June-bug's expression was pensive, just for a moment or so, though there was nothing grudging in it. "I made that shirt for our Wesley, Christmas of '59," she reflected. "He took uncommon pride in his appearance." She sighed. "It's good to see somebody wearing it again."

There was a brief, weighted silence, then the door opened and Jacob came in. The children, apparently, had already left for school, as there was no sign of them anywhere about.

"Well, now," the stationmaster said, looking Parrish over, "you cleaned up beyond my best expectations."

Savannah laughed, though secretly she was thunderstruck at the change in the doctor's appearance. He was devilishly good-looking, for one thing, and carried himself with a sort of unconscious confidence in his own strength and abilities, a quality she had not seen in him before. Although she was still wary of him, she could admit, at least to herself, that she might have underestimated the man.

June-bug rounded him up and shooed him to the table, like a mother hen gathering in a stray chick, and he sat down, remarkably, and looked at the plate of flapjacks she put in front of him.

"Eat," June-bug commanded. "You look peaky."

Savannah was past due at the Brimstone Saloon, where she hoped to meet up with Trey and hammer out some sort of work schedule, and she imagined Jacob had plenty of chores to do, yet they both lingered, curious about this stranger. It was almost as though someone vaguely resembling the doctor had slipped in during the night to take his place.

Parrish sighed, picked up his fork, and took a cautious bite. Then he took another, and another one after that. It was somehow a momentous occasion, although Savannah could not have said why such a thing could be. When the doctor became aware that everybody was watching him, he looked a little indignant, and both Savannah and Jacob averted their eyes.

Determined to put the day to good use, Savannah went into her rented bedroom to reclaim her handbag, then set out resolutely for the Brimstone Saloon. It didn't take long to reach the place, since it was only a hundred yards or so down the rutted track that passed as a road. The brave little schoolhouse stood just opposite, reminding Savannah of an underling pitched to fling itself upon some brutish bully.

She wondered whose brilliant idea it had been to build two such institutions face-to-face that way, and decided within the confines of that self-same thought that it didn't matter to her. After all, there they were, set solid on their foundations, each one holding its ground.

It was both a disappointment and a relief to Savannah that there were no children playing in the overgrown grass surrounding the school. She loved kids, but she'd learned a long time ago to be careful about speaking to them, at least in the presence of their parents. Too often, the mother or father would drag the child back from her, as though she were some sort of monster, ready to pounce, or the carrier of some dread disease.

So, with a faint and familiar sadness weighting her heart, Savannah turned her back on the school and stood looking up at the building into which she'd sunk every cent she'd saved over the ten years since she'd sung her first song in a saloon. She was good with money, and not overly fond of trinkets and geegaws like a lot of the women she'd known, and for those reasons, she'd managed to put by a good deal. She'd made wise investments, too.

She rested her hands on her hips, surveying her plain clapboard purchase, with its swinging doors and hitching rails and the glass windows that were bound to be broken in the first good brawl. What, she wondered, in a state of sudden and keen despair, had she been thinking of, tying up her life savings in such an enterprise?

Savannah sighed. It hadn't been Trey Hargreaves, though God knew, he was everything a man ought to be, and then some. No, try as she might, she'd never come to care for Trey, except as a friend, and that had probably been fortunate, since he'd felt pretty much the same way about her.

Just then, the doors swung open and Trey came out onto the wooden sidewalk, grinning that grin that had set so many female hearts to fluttering, from there to Choteau and probably well beyond.

"It's about time you got here, pardner," he said. He wore a tailored coat, even though it was full summer— a hundred shades of green and yellow were daubed against the distant timber like paint—and the temperature was someplace north of hot. There wasn't a drop of sweat on him. His shirt was white and fancy, and his vest was a rich blue brocade, with a gold watch chain dangling from the pocket. Black, well-fitting trousers and shiny boots completed the picture. "I pour a good glass of whiskey, but my singing voice ain't exactly memorable."

Savannah smiled at her friend. "On the contrary," she retorted, "nobody who heard you sing would ever be able to forget the experience, try though they might."

He laughed as he crossed the sidewalk, his boot heels resounding against the new, raw wood. Reaching her, he took her shoulders in his hands and stooped to plant a brotherly kiss on her forehead.

"Come and meet my wife," he said, and started to pull her toward the schoolhouse.

Savannah balked. "Now?"

"Yes, now," he replied, with mock impatience.

"Won't we be interrupting?"

Trey narrowed those legendary silver eyes of his. "What burr's gotten under your saddle?" he wanted to know.

Savannah's throat ached. She looked up toward the station and then toward the springs, which lay in the other direction, and saw that no help was likely to come from either. "Trey, I'm a saloon woman," she reminded him, in an anxious whisper. "There are folks who'd be real upset to learn I'd been in the same room with their children—"

Trey gave her arm a gentle jerk to get her moving again. "Well, to hell with them, if that's their attitude," he said. "Come on. You're going to like Rachel. Just a little bit of a thing, but she's sure got me buffaloed."

Savannah bit into her lower lip, but she allowed herself to be pulled across the road, through the deep, fragrant Montana grass, up the step to the schoolhouse door. Trey knocked lightly, and all too soon, the rough-board panel swung back on creaking hinges, revealing a small, dark-haired woman with exquisite features and a gleam of intelligence in her eyes.

"Rachel," Trey announced proudly, "this is my partner, Savannah Rigbey. Savannah, my wife."

To say that Rachel was surprised would not have sufficed to describe the expression that crossed her face, however momentarily. Trey, damn his insensitive masculine hide, had neglected to tell his bride that his business associate was a woman, that much was vividly clear. Savannah was mortified; her knees felt watery and conversely, she wanted to turn and flee toward the hills, which was downright silly since she'd done nothing wrong. Not where Trey Hargreaves was concerned, at least.

"Hello," Rachel said, and put out one small, cool hand.

Savannah nodded. "Hello," she said lamely. "I know you're busy with your students, so I'll just go—" She turned on her heel, but Trey took another hold on her elbow and held her fast.

"I hope you'll join us for supper tonight," Rachel Hargreaves said. "Say, six o'clock?"

Savannah's breath had gone shallow. She was not used to being invited to supper, and had nearly forgotten how one responded to such requests. "Well," she murmured.

"She'll be there," Trey told his wife, with a smile, and a look passed between the two of them that fairly crackled. Even Savannah, a mere bystander, felt the flash of heat.

Rachel gave her husband's partner one last thoughtful glance, nodded, and closed the door.

"You didn't tell her!" Savannah accused, in an angry hiss, as the two of them crossed the street again, headed for the saloon.

"Tell her what?" Trey asked, and he looked and sounded genuinely confused.

"That I'm a woman! Damn it, you lunkhead, you don't just spring something like that on a person!"

Trey chuckled, but he still seemed mildly baffled. "I told her I had a partner, coming in from Choteau. She didn't ask any questions."

"That's because she naturally assumed I was a man," Savannah sputtered. "She was probably expecting some portly fellow with a gold incisor, a big cigar, and a bald spot!"

Trey laughed at that image and, since they had gained the doors of the saloon, reached out to hold one open so she could step in ahead of him. Although there were no horses or wagons out front, the place was doing a surprisingly good business, especially for so early in the day. Savannah didn't know whether to feel chagrined or encouraged by the fact.

"You're worried that Rachel will be jealous of you," Trey said, in a booming voice that made everyone from the bartender to the brooding drifter by the back wall look up, and thus brought stinging color to Savannah's cheeks. "Don't give that another thought. She knows I'm downright foolish over her."

Out of the corner of one eye, Savannah saw the hefty bartender, who was busily wiping out a glass, indulge in the sparest of smiles.

She flung out her hands and let them slap against her sides in exasperation. "I give up," she said. "Just don't blame me if she starts peeling the hide off you the minute she gets you alone."

Trey looked damnably confident of his wife's adoration. "It isn't my hide——"

Savannah cut him off. "Don't you dare say it."

He laughed again, and let his eyes drift over her prim

shirtwaist and skirts. "You aren't planning to sing and socialize in that outfit, are you? Seems to me it would be better suited to pouring tea."

Savannah lowered her voice, and her hands found their way back to her hips. "I don't need you or any other man to tell me what to wear when I conduct business, Trey Hargreaves. Furthermore, you'd better remember that I'm not selling anything but whiskey!"

Trey raised both eyebrows and both hands. "Whoa," he said. "All I meant was, I've been running this place by myself ever since it was built, and I've got a house to put up before it snows." He grinned, cocky with pride. "It's one of those sent-for places. Coming by train and freight wagon, all the way from Seattle."

Again, Savannah felt a strange stab of something she wasn't sure she wanted to identify: sorrow, loneliness—envy?

"Soon as the house is finished," Trey went on, when she didn't speak, "you can have the rooms upstairs."

Savannah raised her eyes to the ceiling. Oh, joy, she thought ruefully. An apartment over a saloon in a three-building town. In one and the same moment, though, she wondered what she'd expected. This was her life—saloons and rooms above them, gaudy dresses and singing to the strains of tinny pianos, sawdust on the floors. Nothing was ever going to change, not for her.

Jacob McCaffrey set the checkerboard down in the middle of one of the tables with a thump that should have served as a warning to Pres, but it didn't. "What do you say we make things interesting?" the older man asked, taking a seat on the bench opposite. "Play for pennies."

June-bug was rolling out piecrusts nearby, her shining eyes watchful and intent. "Jacob McCaffrey, you know very well that I don't hold with wagerin'. And here you are, a man of God."

Jacob passed Pres a humorous, beleaguered, and masterfully subtle look. "Now, June-bug," he replied, already lining out the round, red checker pieces in front of Pres with a rhythmic clatter reminiscent of horses' hooves on cobblestone. "It's just a sociable little game, between me and the doc here. The good Lord don't take issue with the like of that."

"We'll see what you have to say when you find yourself playin' checkers with the devil himself," June-bug huffed, using extra force as she wielded her wooden rolling pin, although both her tone and countenance fell a little short of full conviction.

"If the Lord's going to throw a body into hell for bettin' pennies on a round of checkers," Jacob reasoned philosophically, aligning his own pieces on their proper squares, "then He and I probably wouldn't get on together anyhow."

Pres stifled a smile. He'd long since decided that God was either hostile or totally disinterested in His own creation, if indeed He existed at all, but Jacob's homespun faith was a lot easier to take than that of the Bible pounders and raging exhorters he'd encountered in other places. He laid the last of his money on the table, fool that he was, and after an hour or so of long,

ponderous silences between careful moves, Jacob had
relieved him of that *and* the stagecoach ticket.

The stationmaster wasn't about to offer a rematch.
He just put away the red and black pieces, folded the
board, and gave Pres what was probably meant to pass as
a grin.

"Guess you'll just have to stay on here at Springwater," he said. Then he got up and walked off, and all
Pres could do was stare after him. Damned if he hadn't
been had.

CHAPTER

3

SAVANNAH WAS ALONE in the little room behind June-bug McCaffrey's cookstove, a colorful tangle of silks and satins covering the bed before her like flowers tumbled from a garden basket. None of the gowns was suitable for dinner at Rachel Hargreaves's table, even if the woman *did* live above a saloon, and yet Savannah chafed at the idea of playing the lady by attending the meal in her tidy skirt and shirtwaist. Her sins were many, by her own assessment, let alone that of society in general, but an attitude of pretense did not number among them.

She frowned, tapping her chin as she considered the garments. The blue one was probably the most innocuous, with its wild spill of ruffles and rhinestone buttons, though the neckline was too low and the skirt hemmed only to midcalf. If she wore that, Rachel would think she was after her husband for certain, and that would not serve. The yellow was bright to the point of being brazen, the green flattered her hair and complexion, but left her back bare, except for a lattice pattern of grosgrain ribbon. The garnet plunged in front, and though the resulting V was filled in with black lace, the outfit seemed to bring out the worst in even the best of men. Whenever Savannah wore it, she made a point of carrying the derringer as well, tucked away in a hidden pocket.

A light tap on the framework of the door caused her to turn, a little startled. Emma was standing in the opening, her brown eyes wide as she took in the dresses. The child let out a long, wondrous breath. "Silk?" she whispered, as though barely daring to murmur the word.

Savannah nodded. Emma, like most frontier children, had probably never seen anything but buckskin, rough-spun woolens, and calico. "Satin, too," she said. "Would you like to touch them?"

Emma came forward tentatively, stood for a moment with the color of the dresses seeming to reflect off her face like light from a stained glass window, then stretched out a small brown hand. Her fingers were trembling slightly as she drew back, in a sudden motion, well short of the glimmering fabrics.

"You won't do them any harm, Emma," Savannah said, putting an arm lightly around the child's erect, solid little shoulders. "Go ahead."

With renewed courage, though visibly holding her breath, Emma reached out again, caressed one dress and then another, with a slow reverence that touched the warm, bruised place at the very center of Savannah's long-hardened heart.

"So pretty," Emma marveled, in the tones of one offering a solemn prayer. "Like a cardinal's feathers, or a blue jay's . . ."

"Indeed," put in a masculine voice from behind them, "the plumage of a veritable bird of paradise, brightly colored, singing the sweetest of songs and none other."

Savannah whirled, though she had known that it was Dr. Parrish she would find, looking on. He was leaning with one shoulder braced against the door frame, his arms folded, his expression one of kindly disdain. She felt blood rise into her face and damned herself for reacting to him at all. "I do believe there is an insult hidden away in that statement somewhere," she said, keeping her tones even for the sake of the child. "What a pity that I care so little for your opinion, sir."

He did not move from his indolent position, but merely raised his eyebrows. "An insult? Perish the thought," he said. "Methinks you are too prickly by half, Miss Rigbey. That is the proper form of address, isn't it? 'Miss Rigbey'?"

She'd never married; the scandal had ruined her chances. Burke Eldon—well, she didn't even like to think about him, about what a mistake it had been to believe in him. About what she'd sacrificed.

Still, all of that had happened so long ago, so far away, and it wasn't as if she'd been the first woman to be badly used. It was past time to forget and move on, though it wasn't easy doing that. "Yes," she said, with all the dignity she could summon. "'Miss' will do just fine."

Emma, emboldened by Savannah's invitation to touch the dresses, had taken up the blue one and was holding it in front of her flat little bosom, clearly trying to imagine herself grown up and clad in something so grand. Savannah grabbed hold of the present moment and held on, but the pit of her stomach was quivering and she wasn't entirely certain she wouldn't be sick. Forgetting wasn't so easy, of course—the pain, the shame, the fear, the fury, all of it was still with her. "Do you make a practice, sir, of entering a lady's private refuge without so much as a by-your-leave?"

Emma watched with new interest, though no discernible alarm, looking from one adult to the other.

Parrish inclined his magnificent head in a sham of abeyance. "My apologies," he said. "Miss June-bug sent me to ask if you'd like to take a bottle of her elderberry wine along to supper tonight. She'd have come to make the inquiry herself, I expect, but she's busy outside, helping Jacob put salve on a lame horse."

Savannah considered, then nodded in the affirmative. She did not indulge in wine, indeed did not take spirits of any kind, but without June-bug's offering, she would have to present herself empty-handed that evening. She hated being obliged, even for something as ordinary as supper.

The doctor's gaze strayed over the jewel-toned tousle of dresses on the mattress. "Wear the red one," he had the audacity to suggest. Then, while she was still foundering and flailing, awash in a strange, sweet aggravation, he pushed gracefully away from the woodwork, turned, and strolled off.

"I like him," Emma confided.

Savannah sighed. "That brings the count to one," she said wearily.

"Oh, no," Emma disagreed, her dark eyes serious and bright. "Jacob likes him, and so does Miss June-bug. They say he'll be living at Springwater from now on— he just doesn't know it yet."

Savannah couldn't help smiling at that, though Dr. Parrish had left her feeling like a bird flapping its wings under a bonnet. She hoped it didn't mean what she thought it did, because after Burke, she'd sworn never to trust, let alone care about, another man.

In the end, she wore the skirt and shirtwaist she'd had on all day, somewhat to Pres's disappointment, actually, since he'd hoped for at least a glimpse of her in that red confection with the black lace. Instead, though, she went hurriedly through the main room of the station, a basket over one arm, a loose-yarned shawl around her shoulders. In the basket, of course, was June-bug's elderberry wine, discreetly covered by a checkered table napkin.

"Trey'll walk you back home, I reckon," June-bug commented. She was standing beside the front door as Savannah advanced upon it, and looking a bit fretful. You'd have thought Springwater was the heart of some crime-ridden metropolis instead of a mere wide spot along a remote cattle trail. "I don't think you ought to be out alone after it gets dark."

Savannah smiled and at that Pres looked away quickly, annoyed at what it made him feel—like Lazarus coming awake in the tomb. He'd deadened his emotions on purpose, after all, and he wanted them to stay that way. His gaze immediately locked with that of Jacob, who was standing in his usual post before the hearth, unlighted pipe in hand. Miss June-bug did not allow the use of tobacco in her presence, though she had been known, it was reported, to take a measure of dandelion or elderberry wine on the occasion of communion or if her arthritic knees got to paining her beyond bearing.

Pres brought his mind back to his own problems. He was effectively stranded, thanks to Jacob McCaffrey's cutthroat skill at checkers, with nothing to call his own except the battered leather bag his father had left him. Even the proverbial clothes on his back belonged to someone else—his own had disappeared mysteriously, to be burned, he suspected, in Miss June-bug's cooking fire. His money was gone, and so was the stagecoach, which had passed through on schedule early that afternoon, and set out again as soon as the driver had partaken of a meal and Jacob and Toby had exchanged fresh horses for spent ones. Up until the moment the coach thundered off over the rutted track, Pres had half-expected the old man to return the ticket so he could move on. Instead, he'd made a subtle show of tearing it up and tossing it into the cold grate.

Pres pushed away from the table, agitated almost

beyond his endurance, and began to tread back and forth like a fidgety horse looking for a break in the fence-line. By that time, Savannah had gone, taking those vague, joyful stirrings she'd roused in him away with her, mercifully. The children, Christabel, Emma, and young Toby, were outside, playing some noisy game. The Leebrook girl and her baby, both restless through the day, were resting quietly, and June-bug had returned to the stove, now wholly absorbed in preparing supper for her acquired brood. Many women would have been frazzled in her position, and justifiably so, but she seemed to thrive on cooking and generally "doing for" a houseful of people.

"Good thing we ain't got a rug," Jacob observed. His mouth was as somber as ever, but there was a glint of humor in his eyes. "You'd wear a hole right through it, pacing to and fro that way."

Pres stopped, his hands resting on his hips, and glowered. "I suppose you've got a better suggestion?"

Jacob actually smiled, though so briefly that Pres almost wondered if he'd imagined it. "Matter of fact, I do. You could ride up to the Johnson place and have a look at Granny's rheumatiz. Miss June-bug says it torments her night and day."

Rheumatism. After the things he'd seen, after the battles and their horrendous aftermaths, such a trifling malady would be a lark. "Hot packs," he said distractedly. "All she needs are hot packs and maybe a little— a very little—laudanum."

"Havin' a real doctor come to call would probably go a long way towards making Granny feel better," Jacob persisted, as though Pres hadn't already outlined a method of treatment for the old woman's affliction. "The idea of it, you know."

Pres thrust out a long sigh. In the first place, he didn't know where the 'Johnson place' was, and in the second, he didn't have a horse. He'd lost a first-rate gelding at faro, back in Choteau, further proof of his sorry situation. *Pres*, he thought, furious with himself, with fate, and with Jacob McCaffrey, *you've done the home folks proud.*

"I'll take you up to Granny's shack tomorrow," Jacob announced, when Pres didn't speak. "Provided things are under control around here, that is."

"I suppose it's too much to hope that you'll give back my money if I agree?" Pres ventured.

"Way too much," Jacob replied with what passed for affability. "Takes a long while to earn even that much around here. Even for doctorin', you're not likely to get cash money very often. A chicken, maybe, or a mess of trout. A bag of turnips or potatoes. Yes, sir, it could be some time before you've got the wherewithal to put Springwater behind you for good. Course, June-bug and I will have to charge for your room and board, but you can work that off here at the station, grooming horses and the like. I ain't as spry as I once was."

Pres's jaw clamped down so hard that relaxing it again took a concentrated act of will. It wasn't being expected to earn his keep that irritated him—he'd done that, one way or another, ever since he left home for medical college—no, it was the way Jacob had gotten the better of him with hardly any effort at all.

Inside, Pres was chasing his tail like a fox stitched up in a burlap sack. He had that Lazarus feeling again, and his spirit was raw, having been atrophied for so long. "I can manage that," he said. "I'll sleep in the barn, though, and I don't eat much."

Jacob assessed Pres's lean frame and then focused that dark, somber gaze on his face again. "The loft's still warm enough for a man to take his rest in of a night," he allowed, "though the first frost could come at any time, summer or none. As for the food, well, it takes victuals to run a man's body just the way it takes coal to power a steam engine. I reckon most of your sustenance has been comin' out of a bottle, the last little while. Time that stopped."

While Pres would not have brooked such familiarity, such downright presumption, from anyone else, he had little choice in this instance. He was broke, literally and figuratively, with no horse, no stagecoach ticket, and no particular place to go anyway. Inside, he was one big bruise. He might as well come to final ruination in Springwater, he figured, as anywhere else.

"You may come to regret forcing me to stay here," he said evenly.

Jacob spared what might have been a smile on a less craggy and austere face than his. "I don't reckon I will at that," he said. "Come along. I'll show you to the loft and lay out your chores while Miss June-bug finishes makin' our supper. First thing in the morning, we'll head up to Granny Johnson's."

Pres wanted to pick up something heavy and throw it, but he didn't give in to the impulse. Instead, he just followed Jacob out of the station and around back, to the stables, where it looked like he would be sleeping and working for the rest of his natural life.

Rachel had gotten out her lace tablecloth for the occasion of Savannah's visit, and there were tapers flickering in the pair of brass candlesticks set on either side of a bowl brimming with fresh, fragrant wildflowers. Various lamps had been lit as well and the place smelled pleasantly of roasted fowl of some sort, turnips mashed with butter, and fresh biscuits. All of it would go well with the wine.

Trey, proud as any peacock, welcomed Savannah, taking the basket and her shawl, and Rachel, his schoolteacher wife, smiled as she untied her apron and came away from the small potbelly stove where she had evidently prepared all or most of the meal. There was not so much as a trace of dislike or disapproval in Rachel's eyes as she approached; happiness overflowed from her, an excess of the stuff, warm as firelight. Savannah had a desolate, shut-out feeling, just for a moment there.

"Do sit down," Rachel said, taking both Savannah's hands in hers and clasping them warmly. "It is such a treat to have a guest!"

Trey had already opened the wine bottle and set it on the table, between covered dishes with fragrant steam escaping at their edges. He drew back Savannah's chair, and then his wife's. Only when they were both settled, with their napkins in their laps, did he take his own seat. Savannah was secretly amazed at the changes in him, and meant to nettle him a little for his pretty manners, once they were out of Rachel's hearing. The first time Savannah had met Trey, he'd gotten himself hauled off to the hoosegow for riding his horse right through the front doors of the Two-holer Saloon in Missoula and nearly trampling two Temperance workers there to turn the revelers from their wicked ways. Now, he was almost a gentleman.

"Trey's going to start on the foundation for our house tomorrow morning," Rachel confided, when they were all enjoying the succulent food. There was a flush in her cheeks and a glow in her eyes when she looked at her husband that bespoke tender affection and, at the same time, an almost ungovernable passion. "What a fine thing it will be, to have Emma living with us again. We'll have a proper kitchen, too, with a proper stove, and a genuine bathing room—"

Savannah envied Trey's wife, envied her mightily, and not just for having such a grand house forthcoming. No, it was the prospect of a *home* that Savannah coveted, a family, a life that might be considered at least remotely normal. Back east, it would have been highly indecorous for a married woman to hold a schoolteacher's position, and Trey, as a saloon proprietor, would have been assigned a very low social status indeed. Here, though, in the west, where new traditions were taking shape, Trey and Rachel might well be considered respectable.

Quite a contrast, Savannah thought, with her own future. She, who could expect to be viewed as a prostitute unto the end of her days.

The injustice of it made her want to weep, but there was no profit in that. She couldn't go back, after all, couldn't smooth out the twists and turns in the path she'd trod, nor level the steep decline that had brought her to this time and place and state of affairs. She was what she was, and she'd make the best of it, just as she had always done.

"I'll take over here tomorrow," she said, when the evening was nearly over, referring, of course, to the saloon business downstairs. Trey had done his hitch and more, and deserved the necessary time to dig the foundation for the house he would share with Rachel, Emma, and the other children that were bound to come along sooner or later.

Sooner, Savannah thought, if she wasn't misreading that certain ephemeral quality in Rachel's eyes. She'd seen it before, though mostly in far less pleasant circumstances—her midwife grandmother had taught her what to look for, when they'd both hoped Savannah would follow in her footsteps—and it always meant there was a baby brewing, whether the mother had been so advised or not.

"Trey will see you safely home," Rachel said, when the dishes had been cleared and they had sat awhile, sipping coffee. At the door, when Trey was halfway down the outside staircase, she laid a hand to Savannah's arm and spoke in a soft voice. "I'm so glad you've come to Springwater, Savannah. I know we'll be friends."

Not for the first time since her arrival, Savannah felt tears of emotion threaten. She'd acquired numerous male confidants throughout her life, Trey being the best of them, but women tended to dislike and distrust her. She didn't blame them—surely they could not be expected to invite a saloon woman into their homes for tea parties and quilting bees—but she had suffered for her exclusion. Now, here was Rachel Hargreaves, a schoolteacher, educated and gently raised, wanting to befriend her.

She sighed inwardly. Rachel might be of a very different opinion, once she'd seen her husband's business partner in one of her jewel-colored dresses, all of them scandalous by anyone's reckoning, with her hair done up in beads and feathers and her face painted. No doubt the words of her songs would drift up through the floorboards as well, borne on the tinkling notes of the cheap piano below, naughty tunes, designed to inspire devilment in dry-throated cowboys, and maudlin ones, offering cheap solace to the lonely, the bereaved, the defeated.

"I would like that," Savannah said, in parting. "To be your friend, I mean." She meant it, every word, but even then she held out little hope that it would ever be so.

Trey took her arm and guided her down the steep wooden steps behind the saloon. Through the thin plank walls, they heard the click of billiard balls and a swell of rough talk. A half dozen cowboys had ridden in, late that afternoon, and Trey had left them in the care of the bartender.

"I could change my clothes and come back," Savannah suggested, feeling guilty for leaving so much of the burden on him. He'd built the place, after all, and run it almost single-handedly ever since.

"Tomorrow'll be soon enough," Trey said. There was no moon, just the faintest curved etching against the dark sky, and he carried a kerosene lantern in one hand. "Rachel was glad of your company," he went on. "She's been fussing over that pitiful little stove of ours since she closed down the schoolhouse for the day. It's lonely out here a lot of the time, especially for a woman."

"Surely June-bug has been cordial."

Trey chuckled. "Miss June-bug is always cordial," he answered. "She's busy, though, forever cooking or sweeping or looking after some spindly-legged chick she's taken under her wing. Rachel's closest friend, Evangeline Wainwright, lives about ten miles east of town, but they don't see each other very often, given the distance."

Savannah kept pace with the edge of the circle of light cast by Trey's lantern. "I like your wife, Trey," she said truthfully. "Rachel is a fine person, bright-minded as anybody I've ever come across. But I'm not the sort of woman she's looking to keep company with. She was only trying to be polite, that's all."

Trey stopped, raised the lantern, and peered down into Savannah's face. She blinked, bedazzled, in the wash of light.

"Just what sort of woman do you reckon yourself to be?" he demanded. He didn't know about the night she'd run off with Burke, thinking they were going to be married and live out a happy succession of golden days and weeks, months and years, as true partners. What a naive little fool she'd been, taking fairy tales for gospel.

She smiled, touched by his fierce loyalty. He truly liked her. Still, he was a man, and she had always gotten along well with the masculine gender. Until Dr. Prescott Parrish, that is; the two of them struck sparks, metal against metal. If that was "getting along," that excitement, that quivering rush in the pit of her stomach, it was damn scary. "There is a perception that goes with working in a saloon, Trey. You know that. It's all right for you—it just makes you a bit of a rogue, but for me it's a very different matter. I sing in barrooms. I sell whiskey to people who would probably be better off without it." *I was misled by a man I trusted, even looked up to, and my own father turned me out of his house.* She sighed. "It's just assumed that I do other things, too."

Trey spat a curse. "If anybody dares to say that, I'll flatten their nose with the back of a shovel," he said. He sounded sincere.

Savannah laughed, though in truth she felt more like weeping, because of what she remembered, and because what she wanted to be was such a far cry from what she was. "That would change nothing at all," she pointed out. "Come along, Trey—I've got to get back to the station. There'll be talk about you and me soon enough as it is, without our dallying in the dark to lend credence to the gossip."

Trey was scowling, but he started walking again, toward the golden squares of light that were the windows of Springwater station. "You suppose Jacob'll be able to talk that sorry-looking doc into staying on?" he asked, when they were almost to the porch.

Savannah felt the strangest urge to defend Parrish, to say that he was really quite presentable, now that he'd had a bath and a good night's sleep, but she stopped herself. It wasn't her task in life to smooth that scoundrel's way; she had both hands full just looking after her own affairs and, truth to tell, she wasn't exactly assuring herself an honored place in history.

"He'll stay on awhile," she answered, as they gained the base of the station house steps. "He lost his horse at faro, back in Choteau, and this morning Jacob checkered him out of his money and a stagecoach ticket."

"We could use a doctor around here," Trey allowed. Savannah wondered if he was imagining Rachel, months from then, laboring to bear his child, but of course she wouldn't have asked for anything. She and Trey were close friends, but not *that* close.

"He conducted himself well enough yesterday, when Miranda gave birth," she said. "He was sober at the time, but who knows how long that will last?" In her mind, she saw the doctor at the Hell-bent Saloon, consuming whiskey like he was feeding a fire in his belly. Or dousing one in his soul.

Trey's face was craggy with shadows in the rising light of his lantern. "He didn't take so much as a swallow when he came into the Brimstone today. Just sat there, staring at the wall like he could see through it to some other place. I tried to strike up a conversation, but he didn't have much to say. Just his name, as I recall."

Savannah mounted the first step. Through the

station's thick log walls, she could hear Miranda's baby crying. The sound was lusty and somehow heartening, for all that it was an ordinary thing. "You can go back home now, Trey. I believe I'd like to stay out here for a few minutes and gather in my thoughts."

"You're all right, aren't you?" Trey sounded genuinely worried, in the way a protective elder brother might have been. "It can take a lot out of a person, that stage trip from Choteau. Why, when Rachel came, the coach nearly turned over in Willow Creek, and I had to go out and fetch her ashore on horseback."

Savannah smiled again, clasping a lodge pole hitching rail in her hands and looking up at the black sky, where a few faint stars winked and twinkled. The wind was rising, promising a storm; the portent of lightning was a silent reverberation in the hot air. "I'm just fine, Trey. Go home to your wife." She'd thanked them both for a pleasant evening, and so did not press the matter of her gratitude. "I'll see you tomorrow morning."

Trey hesitated a moment, then glanced toward the saloon, no doubt thinking of Rachel, awaiting him in their rustic rooms upstairs. It was enough, evidently, to propel him toward home. "Good night," he said, as he moved away, the lantern light swinging easily at his side.

"So that's your partner," said Prescott Parrish, from the darkness behind her.

Savannah was so startled that she nearly swallowed her tongue. She turned, one hand to her breast in an unconscious attempt to slow her heartbeat down to a reasonable pace, to see him materialize out of the gloom like some sort of specter. "I despise a sneak, Dr. Parrish," she snapped, when fury and fear made way for speech. "How dare you lurk in the shadows and eavesdrop on a private conversation?" *How dare you have such a frightening effect on me?*

He chuckled and had the out-and-out temerity to stand right beside her, there on the McCaffreys' porch, one shoulder braced against a supporting pole. "I wasn't lurking," he said. "I came around the corner from the barn and heard you discussing me. Naturally, the topic was of interest."

Savannah blushed to remember the nature of that conversation, and most of the steam went out of her. "All the same, announcing yourself would have been the gentlemanly thing to do."

His teeth flashed white in the darkness. She could see him now, in the light coming from the window behind them, if only as a shadow towering over her. "Ah, but there you have it, Miss Rigbey. I am not a gentleman, and therefore cannot be expected to behave as one."

Savannah stood her ground. "On the contrary," she said, "you were *born* a gentleman. And if you do not behave as such, it is not for want of training. I think you choose to be obnoxious. You're angry and you mean to make the world suffer for all your petty grievances."

He leaned in very close, and she smelled soap and clean water on his skin, but no hint of whiskey, stale or otherwise. "I do not recall asking for your opinion," he said pointedly. "But since you gave it so readily, I will reciprocate with my own. You, Miss Rigbey, are no lady. Since I am no gentleman, we ought to suit each other just fine."

They just stood there, the two of them, for the longest time. The air seemed awash with liquid lightning, and Savannah's heart was beating so fast that she feared it would race right out of her throat and leave her behind.

He reached up, touched her mouth with the tip of an idle index finger. "What's happening here?" he murmured, and he might have been talking to himself, the mountains, or the moon as much as to Savannah, given his distracted tone.

His touch seemed to sear her, through and through. She didn't have an answer, and so didn't offer one. Nor did she move away, flee into the station as a decent woman would have done.

At last, and very slowly, like a man making his way through a dream, he took Savannah's shoulders in his hands, pulled her close, and lowered his mouth to hers for a long, softly tempestuous kiss.

She supposed she should have struggled—kicked—slapped—something. But she didn't. She just stood there, letting him kiss her, kissing him back, and enjoying the whole experience. When it was over, and he fairly tore his lips from hers, she might actually have swooned if he hadn't still been holding on to her shoulders. She had reveled in the exchange, indeed, she wanted more, but she would have died before admitting as much. In point of fact, all she could do was stare up at him, astounded.

His dark eyes glittered in the thin light. Somewhere

in the distance, thunder boomed, and the horizon seemed to tilt at a wild angle as lightning flashed. If she hadn't known better, Savannah would have sworn she'd just kissed the devil himself.

He smiled at her, almost insolently, then turned and walked off into the night, whistling under his breath.

Savannah took a few moments to breathe deeply, in the hope of calming her heart and letting the blush in her cheeks fade a little, then went inside the station. Jacob and June-bug were seated in their rocking chairs, facing the evening fire, June-bug holding the newborn baby gently in her arms.

"There you are," she said, in a quiet voice that held music even when she wasn't singing. "Did Trey walk you home?"

Savannah summoned up a smile as she set down the now-empty basket and removed her shawl. Inside, she was trembling, and she could still feel Parrish's mouth on hers, at once conquering and surrendering. Forceful, yet totally unlike the way Burke had kissed her. "Yes, he did. Rachel is a lovely woman, and quite a good cook."

June-bug nodded and crooned something to the sleeping infant. "She's made all the difference in the world to Trey, and to Emma, too. I suppose she's all excited about that new house of hers."

Jacob ruminated on his wife's remark for a few moments, then joined in the conversation. "I didn't figure they'd get it here before spring. Maybe they oughtn't to get their hopes up, Rachel and Trey."

"Nonsense," June-bug said, in a tone of mild reproach. "Seattle isn't that far. Those freight wagons will be here any day now. Just you wait and see."

Jacob's response was typically good-natured and dry as sun-bleached bones. "I hope you're right, Miss June-bug," he said. "I surely do."

Thunder sounded again, closer now, and June-bug raised worried eyes to the ceiling. "You ought to fetch the doc inside, Jacob. He's liable to catch his death, sleepin' out yonder in the barn on a night like this."

Jacob might have smiled; it would have been hard to tell, even in good light. "Never you mind," he said. "Never you mind. Young Dr. Parrish is right where he ought to be."

CHAPTER

4

IT WAS STILL EARLY—the air was chilly as the inside of a spring-house in January and the sky was pearl-gray, shot with a watery apricot, above the lacework tangle of evergreens and deciduous trees rimming the horizon. There was a carpet of pine needles and last year's leaves on the ground. Jacob, riding beside Pres's borrowed mare on a fractious old mule he called Nero, pointed out a faint curl of smoke higher up in the foothills, amidst the gray-white trunks of birches and alders.

"That would be Granny's place, there yonder," he said. "Leastways we know she's up and around and has her cookin' fire built."

Pres rubbed the back of his neck and refrained from comment.

"There's one thing I ought to warn you about, before we get there," Jacob allowed, after chewing on the thought for a while.

"What would that be?" Pres asked, with deliberate mildness. His patience was short, maybe because laying off whiskey had left his insides raw and empty, with no more substance than a rotted log eaten through by bugs. Maybe because he was being haunted by thoughts of Savannah Rigbey, sure as Hamlet was haunted by his father's ghost. His temples seemed to be trying to reach across his brain and fuse themselves into a single throbbing pulse, and his stomach had shriveled to a dry shell. Had there been anything in it, he'd have long since heaved up the lot.

"Granny's likely to shoot at us," Jacob replied, with no more inflection than if he'd been saying she enjoyed chasing fireflies with a fruit jar in one hand. "Her eyesight ain't too good, and until she recognizes me and old Nero here, she's liable to be unfriendly."

Pres gave a short bark of a laugh, a sound utterly without humor. "Wonderful."

"No cause to worry," Jacob assured him. "She won't aim to kill."

Sure enough, in the next second, a shotgun blast rent the sky, sending birds flapping and squawking from the trees and small animals skittering through the underbrush.

"You jest hold it right there!" warned a thin, wavery voice.

Jacob and Pres didn't have to draw up on the reins— Jacob had to fight Nero to keep him from wheeling around and laying tracks back to Springwater, and the mare did a little sideways dance that might have been amusing, if it hadn't been for that crazy old woman up ahead, wielding a gun.

"Now, Granny," Jacob yelled good-naturedly, "put

that thing aside. It's me, Jacob McCaffrey. I've brought a doctor to have a look at your rheumatiz!"

A brief silence followed, then Granny's brittle old voice crackled through the morning chill, spreading itself in a gradually widening web of sound like a hairline fracture in an egg shell. "What sort of doctor?"

Jacob gave Pres a sidelong look, as though assessing him so as to give an honest answer. "The real kind, I reckon, with proper schoolin' and plenty of practice behind him." He waited a heartbeat or two, letting his words sink in. Then he spurred the mule forward. "Now, Granny," he called out, "we're comin'. You put a nick in my hide and you'll have Miss June-bug to deal with, so you just leave off shootin' right now."

Pres was fascinated by the spectacle of a scrawny little woman wielding a gun that was bigger than she was. He wanted, for some ridiculous reason, to laugh out loud.

When it was plain that no more potshots were forthcoming, he persuaded the little mare to follow Jacob's mule, along a narrower, upward-curving path, through clouds of rich green leaves and the clean, Christmas-scent of fir trees.

The old woman stood on the sagging porch of her shack, even smaller than she'd appeared from a distance, a wizened, toothless little creature in a poke bonnet and a dress made of mismatched flour sacks stitched none-too-neatly together. On her tiny left foot she wore a black, lace-up boot, on her right, a slipper of some sort.

Pres met her gaze and held it.

"Granny, this here is Prescott Parrish," Jacob announced. "He's a doctor, like I said. We mean to keep him around Springwater as long as we can."

Granny looked Pres over and apparently found him wanting, judging by the little *harumph* sound she made. He hid a grin and inclined his head slightly.

"Morning, Mrs. Johnson," he said, in respectful tones.

She squinted at him, as though trying to discern his innermost motives, though it was more likely that she simply needed spectacles. "You a Yankee?" she demanded, bristling with suspicion.

Pres heaved a sigh. "No, ma'am. I'm not a Confederate, either. Just a plain American, I guess."

She hobbled forward a few steps,· peering from beneath the wide brim of her bonnet. "I ain't never been seen to by no doctor," she said. "Never had the need. But I reckon if Jacob McCaffrey will keep company with you, you're probably a decent feller."

Pres's natural bent toward the practice of medicine had edged aside his own discomforts; he dismounted, tethered the mare to a sapling that grew beside an old, rusted water pump, and untied his bag, having lashed it to the saddle horn before setting out from Springwater. He stood before Granny, looking up because she was on the step and he was still on the ground, and addressed her bluntly, as he did all his patients. "Have you got the rheumatism all through your system, or just in that foot?" He nodded to indicate her slippered foot.

"My whole right side pains me some," Granny admitted, though grudgingly. "It's a sight worse from my hip on down, though."

Pres nodded again. "Well, let's have a look," he said.

Granny's dried-apple face showed alarm. "You mean, you want to see my bare hide?"

He swallowed a chuckle. "Your virtue is safe with me, Mrs. Johnson. I'm a doctor."

Granny squinted at Jacob, still towering against the lightening sky on the back of that mule. He looked, to Pres, like an Old Testament prophet, a solemn herald of wrath and destruction. "You'll come a-runnin' if I holler for you?" the old lady asked.

To his credit, Jacob cracked a smile. He swung down off the mule's back and tethered both his mount and Pres's to a hitching rail that didn't look strong enough to restrain a spindly-legged calf. "Yup," Jacob said.

Granny pondered. "Well," she said, at long last, "all right, then. You come on in, Doc, and I'll hitch up my skirts."

Pres tossed a wry glance to Jacob over one shoulder, and followed Granny into her cabin. The inside was typical of such places, he supposed, and certainly better than he was used to after four years of improvised military hospitals, set up in everything from open fields to musty tents and appropriated horse barns. There was no bed, just a straw pallet on the floor, with one quilt for a cover, and that so worn that it was colorless, and the stuffing showed through. The woodstove was hardly bigger than a milk bucket, giving off only a promise of heat. Pres caught the unmistakable smell of a chamber pot too long unemptied, underlaid with the musty odor peculiar to elderly recluses like Granny.

"When was the last time you had something to eat?"

he asked, in a deliberately gruff tone that implied she might have feasted on any number of delicacies, had she but chosen to do so. In actual fact, he didn't feel sorry for her, except when it came to the pain of her rheumatism. She seemed happy enough to him, otherwise.

"I been eatin' right along," Granny said, none too graciously. "Miss June-bug McCaffrey was up here recentlike, and she brought me some victuals and made me take them. I just used up the last of 'em this mornin'."

"You like living out here, all by yourself?" Pres said, in what was for him a companionable tone of voice. He heard Jacob out on the porch, caught the tantalizing scent of pipe smoke.

Granny seemed to relax a little. "This here's my home. Ain't lived nowhere else in all the time since I got hitched. I ain't goin' to town, so don't you start in on me about it."

He grinned. "Yes, ma'am," he said. Then he set his medical kit on an upended crate, weathered to gray, and snapped the catch. Something of his father always rose to meet him when he opened it, a scent maybe, too subtle to discern consciously, or the ghost of a faded memory.

"Jacob!" Granny whooped, all of the sudden.

The old man opened the door, though slowly. He and Pres exchanged glances. "What?"

Granny made a shooing motion with one hand. "You can go on," she said. "I've taken a likin' to the doc here. I reckon he's all right."

Jacob's eyes smiled, if his mouth didn't. He nodded. "I'll go and catch one of those chickens out there," he said, pausing on the threshold. "I could put the bird on to stew before the doc and me head back down to Springwater."

"Don't you go slaughterin' one of my layin' hens by mistake, Jacob McCaffrey," Granny warned, peering at her old friend. "You chase down that old red one with the missin' wing."

Pres wanted to laugh, not from derision, not from irony, but for the joy of it, for all the reasons he *used* to laugh, before the titans of the North and the South had driven their children into bloody conflict, leaving him and others like him to attend to the horrific consequences. The memories would always be with him, he knew that; he had absorbed and assimilated them into his very being, like food he'd eaten and air he'd breathed. But, oddly, they seemed more deeply buried in those mundane moments, far less immediate than usual. Maybe it had begun, this deep-seated and mysterious change in him, when he'd delivered Miranda Leebrook's baby, though it more likely had to do with Savannah, and the kiss they'd shared.

"Lie down on that pallet over there," he told Granny quietly, "and let's see that hip of yours."

Jacob pursed his mouth, but his Indian-dark eyes were sparkling as he retreated to assassinate an unsuspecting chicken, closing the door behind him.

Granny gave Pres one more looking-over, then made that *harumph* sound again and hobbled over to the pallet. She lay down on her left side, facing the wall, and hiked up her skirts.

Pres had expected inflammation, but he was unprepared for the degree of swelling he actually found. Granny Johnson weighed about as much as a tobacco pouch full of dried bird bones, and her crepe-paper skin looked fragile enough to crumble into dust at a touch, but the flesh covering her hip and the length of her thigh was distended, hard and hot. The pain, he thought, swallowing a low whistle of exclamation, must have been excruciating.

He yearned, in those moments, for proper supplies—opiates, camphor, and the like, but he was down to a quarter bottle of laudanum and a few tinctures and powders. His equipment consisted of the most basic tools of the trade: scalpels, various needles and catgut for sutures, a stethoscope, a mallet for testing reflexes. A saw. God help him, always and forever, a saw.

"Well?" Granny demanded, fractious again. He didn't blame her, there being no kind of grace in her position. "You through lookin' yet? It ain't like I don't feel the breeze."

Pres smiled and replaced the time-grayed petticoat and tattered skirts as gently as he could. "You have a washtub around this place, Mrs. Johnson?" he asked, when she rolled over and sat up, her bright chicken eyes narrowed. "Something you could bathe in?"

"You remarkin' upon somethin' personal?" she wanted to know.

"I wouldn't think of it," Pres disavowed, though, of

course, he'd been doing precisely that all along. More than Granny's temperament had gone sour; she probably hadn't taken a bar of soap to that leathery hide of hers since before Lincoln left Springfield. "Hot water might ease you a little, let you rest."

"Corn whiskey'll do the same," Granny responded, sitting up and settling her skirts modestly around her. "Don't need no fancy Yankee-fied doctor telling me how to look after myself, neither." She paused, peering at him speculatively. "'Less, of course, you happen to have some corn whiskey in that bag of your'n."

Pres had dealt with much more obdurate types than Granny, and he wasn't afraid to let her know it. Unruffled, he looked her straight in the eye and said, "No whiskey. Furthermore, if I have to haul you down to Springwater and dunk you in hot water myself, I'll do it."

Granny glared at him for a long time before finally settling her feathers. "All right, then," she said. "But if I die of the pneumonia, my passin'll be on your conscience."

Savannah wore the garnet gown with the black lace, that first day as mistress of the Brimstone Saloon, just to get it over with. She painted her face and piled all her hair on top of her head in a saucy tumble of curls, and pulled on fishnet stockings and high-heeled slippers for effect.

The first person she met, leaving her room, was Junebug, who couldn't quite hide her misgivings. Miranda, a surprisingly resilient soul, had already emerged from her confinement, and was sitting at one of the trestle tables, puzzling over an open book.

"Joseph and all his brothers!" June-bug exclaimed softly, upon seeing Savannah, one hand splayed over the bosom of her own modest, everyday dress. It was a brown and white calico print with touches of blue that accented the color of her eyes. "You don't even look like the same *person* as before."

Miranda looked up, then down again, quickly. It was plain enough, though, that she was as startled as June-bug had been.

Savannah could have told her friend—at least, she *hoped* Mrs. McCaffrey was still her friend—that indeed she was looking upon someone quite different from the Savannah she was just beginning to know. It seemed futile to explain that this was merely a costume she wore, for a role she played, in order to earn a living. She could have solved the problem by marrying—she'd had more offers than she could count over the years—but for her, entering into matrimony with a man she didn't love would have been a very real sort of whoring. Besides that, even though she mostly knew better, she was still afraid.

When Savannah didn't speak, couldn't speak, June-bug peered into her face, squinting a little. "You all right?" she asked. "You look as if your knees might be saggin' just a little."

Savannah swallowed. "There are reasons for who—what I am," she finally said, in misery.

June-bug laid a hand on her shoulder, left all but bare by the dress. "I reckon that's true of all of us," she said. "For better and for worse."

Already, the sounds of horses could be heard in the road out front, underlaid by the more distant bawling of cattle. That meant thirsty cowboys, willing to pay for a song or two as well as copious amounts of whiskey. Trey had warned her that large and small herds would be driven through town deep into the fall, there being a plentitude of water at the springs.

Savannah wanted to stay, wanted to pour it all out to June-bug, how Burke had said he loved her, when all the while he was lying, and the law was after him. How her father had blamed her, not Burke, and refused to speak to her until the day he died, and how the grief of it all had killed her grandmother. In the end, though, she couldn't risk it.

"You don't have to do this," June-bug said. "Trey's been runnin' that place right along, and he can go on doin' it." Miranda had closed her book and was no longer even pretending not to listen.

Savannah sighed, then shook her head. "I've got to do my part," she said, as much to herself as to June-bug. "Half the business is mine, after all."

June-bug had taken both Savannah's hands in her own, and she held on to them for a moment longer, dropping them only after a final, fierce squeeze. "Them cowboys, they might not understand about you being a lady," she said softly.

Savannah could have kissed the woman, just for assuming the best the way she had. For believing. "I've dealt with many a cowboy and lived to tell the tale," she answered, with a slight smile. "Most of them are just harmless kids, you know, trying to figure out how to be men." She didn't add that she was carrying the derringer in the pocket hidden among the folds of her dress. She had never shot another human being, man nor boy, and she prayed that the necessity would not arise, but she was ready nonetheless.

"And some are no better'n outlaws," June-bug added. "I've seen bitter, hard-eyed men ridin' with these herds since me and Jacob have been out here. The war done somethin' to their souls, made killin' an everyday matter."

There was nothing Savannah could say to that, for she knew it was true. It would be a hundred years at least, she reckoned, before the scars of the great conflict were properly healed. Maybe longer.

"I've got to go," she said, and turned from June-bug, with a nod to Miranda, turned from quiet pleasures, household tasks like sweeping and cooking and putting food by for winter. From tea-drinking and quilt-stitching and gentle talk. There were tears in her eyes as she set her face for the Brimstone Saloon. Trey was across the road from the station, shovel in hand, digging the foundation for his and Rachel's mail-order house, but Savannah pretended not to see him and went on.

She entered the saloon——*her* saloon——by the front doors, and was greeted by a nod from the bartender and the interested leers of a dozen pimply-faced boys, hardly old enough to wear long pants, let alone drink rotgut whiskey, chew tobacco, and gamble away their paltry wages.

One of them made an audacious whooping sound upon seeing Savannah walk in, and then added a suggestive comment; she sought, found, and advanced upon the culprit with such pride and purpose that he backed up hard against the bar and went right on trying to retreat. His compatriots chuckled among themselves. Color climbed the cowboy's grimy face, and his eyes glittered, as though with fever. His Adam's apple bobbed up to his tonsils and back down again. Savannah felt the weight of the silk-swathed derringer against her hip, but she knew she would not be required to use it. The kid wasn't mean, merely ill mannered, and if she was going to start shooting people for that, she'd soon run out of customers.

"What's your name?" she demanded, hands on her hips.

"J-Jimmy," said the boy. "Jimmy Franks."

"Well, Jimmy Franks," Savannah went on, "it seems to me that your manners leave something to be desired. You'd best address me respectfully from now on, if you don't want me to toss you head first into the horse trough."

The others laughed and, after a nervous interval, during which his face got even redder than before, so did Jimmy. "Yes, ma'am," he said, and doffed his filthy, weather-beaten hat to her.

Savannah winked at the bartender. "Give this man a drink," she said. "On me." With that, she went to the piano, raised the lid, and sat down on the rickety stool with a flounce of her red-ruffled skirts. After flexing her fingers briefly, she began to play a sprightly tune, and then to sing, and soon all the cowboys were singing with her.

When they reluctantly took their leave, sometime in the early afternoon, they were promptly replaced by the men they had relieved. The herd was a constant presence, a low rumble filling the sky with dirt.

Trey came to look in on Savannah just as the changing of the guard was taking place, bringing a sandwich wrapped in a cloth napkin, compliments of June-bug. "Looks like a lively crew," he said, assessing the dirty, travel-worn revelers.

Savannah, seated at the only empty table, with Trey across from her, delicately unwrapped the sandwich. Egg salad, with onions and plenty of butter. She nodded in agreement to Trey's statement and bit in appreciatively. She had not realized, until the food arrived, that she was ravenous.

"You have any trouble with them?" Trey prompted, meaning the cowboys, of course.

Savannah chewed, swallowed, and dabbed at her mouth with the napkin before shaking her head. "They're just a bunch of overgrown boys," she said. "Nobody here I can't handle."

Trey's expression was solemn. "Rachel doesn't think you ought to be left here alone," he said. "I'll come and take over for you in an hour or so, after I've had time to wash up and rest awhile."

Savannah was touched by his concern, and especially by Rachel's, yearning for respectable woman friends as she did, but she was more than equal to a room full of saddle-sore cowboys, rowdy or not, and by her accounting, Trey deserved some time off from the Brimstone. "You just stay away," she ordered good-naturedly, "and give me a chance to get the feel of this place. I sunk a fair bit of money into it, after all, and I'll do my part to run it, with no special favors asked."

Trey's forehead crumpled in a dusty frown. "You sure as hell are a stubborn woman," he said, with a marked lack of admiration.

Savannah laughed. "You've known me for five years, Trey. Are you just now figuring that out? You go ahead and spend the evening with your bride; I can look after our investment just fine on my own."

Trey still seemed doubtful, but he knew a losing battle when he saw one. Usually. "I'll be right upstairs. You need me, you just whack on the ceiling with a cue stick, and I'll come right down."

Savannah smiled at the image. "If you say so," she agreed.

"Sing another song, Miss Savannah," one of the cowboys urged, from the bar, where the whiskey was flowing freely. "Somethin' melancholy."

Savannah rolled her eyes at Trey, but she'd finished as much as she could of the sandwich by that time, and she got up and sashayed over to the piano. It was a part of her performance, that swinging and swishing of silk, and it raised an appreciative cheer from the customers, just like always.

She was midway through her song, a maudlin piece about a silver-haired mother watching the road for her "loving boy Billy," never to return from the war, when Dr. Parrish came in. He seemed to set the very air to churning, just that easy.

The sleeves of his borrowed butternut shirt were rolled up, revealing powerful forearms, and his dark hair was rumpled and, at the same time, sleek, like the wing feathers of some predatory bird. Seeing Savannah in her red dress, face paint, and tousled hairdo, he narrowed his eyes.

Savannah had long since come to terms with the facts of who she was and what she did to earn a livelihood, for the most part anyway, but seeing herself reflected in Parrish's handsome face stung, and that in itself was enough to make her angry.

She played harder and sang louder, pretending to ignore the doctor, but instead watching him out of the corner of one eye. They might have been alone in that saloon, the two of them, for all the attention he paid to the bartender or the flock of hooting cowboys washing trail dust from their throats. He didn't go near the bar but instead came straight toward the piano.

Savannah braced herself, more than ready for a fight, but he stopped short of her and sat down at the nearest table, tumbling a drover into the sawdust when he appropriated a chair. The cowboy scowled, then went off to find another place to sit.

Savannah's voice trembled a little, but her audience didn't seem to care. They cheered uproariously when she launched into an encore. She wanted to look away from Parrish's face, wanted to in the worst way, but he seemed to be holding her gaze by means of some fierce magic, and she could not break the spell. Her own voice faded from her ears, as did all the other sounds of that noisy, smoke-hazed place, and she knew she was still singing only because she could feel the sound resonate in her vocal chords.

When the song ended at last, the cowboys bellowed for more, but Savannah couldn't oblige. She remained a captive, could not turn her eyes from Parrish's face.

After a lot of shouting and toasting, the customers gave up trying to persuade her, at least for a little while, and turned back to their drinking in earnest. The doctor did not move, let alone go to the bar and order a drink, as Savannah would have expected him to do.

When the spell slackened, she managed to rise and make her way through the sawdust to where he sat. He was alone by then; the men who had shared his table were engrossed in a game of faro being played in a far corner of the room.

"Pour you a drink?" Savannah inquired, though she knew he didn't have the money to pay. He'd lost every cent remaining to him playing checkers with Jacob McCaffrey.

He shook his head. "Sit down," he said, just as if he had the right to make demands like that. His voice was quiet, though, as if he was making an effort to be polite.

Savannah sat. She told herself it was because the day had been a long one and she was feeling tired, though the truth was, something about this man's presence electrified her as surely as if she'd laid both hands to a lightning bolt. She could barely breathe. "How was Granny Johnson?" she asked, because she needed to say something. The silence might have stretched on forever if she hadn't, with Parrish just sitting there, staring at her.

He ignored the question. "You oughtn't to be seen in public in such a getup," he said. "I have half a mind to wash that stuff off your face myself."

Heat stung Savannah's throat and forehead, made a hot ache beneath her cheekbones. She was hurt and embarrassed, but he didn't need to know that. She wasn't about to let on that his opinion mattered in the least. "You might just as well try to take soap and water to a singed wildcat," she answered mildly. "You'll come away with half again as many scratches if you try it with me."

He sighed, thrust one graceful, long-fingered hand through his hair. She noticed, oddly, that it trembled only slightly. He was well and truly sober, though for how long was anybody's guess. "You're not a whore," he said. "Are you?"

Had it not been for her pride, that question, coming from him, would have caused Savannah to lay her head down on the gouged top of that saloon table and weep. Still, she held on. Spoke moderately. "I most certainly am not."

He looked her over as though she were one of the curious and thus fascinating specimens he'd surely studied in his medical school laboratory. "Then why in hell do you dress and act like one?" He sounded honestly confused, which only went to show that he was lacking in manners as well as tact.

She drew a measured breath and let it out slowly. It

would do no good to fling herself upon him, screeching and scratching, even though that was precisely what she wanted to do, all of the sudden. She had to live at Springwater, after all, and a tale like that was sure to spread from one crew of drovers to another until it reached the Mexican border, by which time it would have grown to epic proportions. "If you don't like the way I'm dressed, *Doctor,* I invite you to get out of my saloon. I've got songs to sing and whiskey to sell. Unless you're buying, I have nothing more to say to you."

He leaned toward her, his dark eyes snapping. "Well, I've got a few things to say to you," he countered. "You don't belong in this place, and you damn well know it."

She bent toward him, and the red feather skewering the pile of curls on top of her head slipped a little, falling between them. She swiped it aside with an angry gesture, and was even angrier when she spotted a smile hiding at the back of his eyes.

"That's where you're wrong, Dr. Parrish—I do belong here. I own half interest in this place. I've been working in saloons since I was sixteen years old. And I see no need to account to you or anyone else for the choices I've made."

He reached up, plucked the feather out of her hair, examined it as though he expected to see something crawling amidst the downy fluff, and laid it aside on the table. "Sell your share of the business to Hargreaves," he said, as confidently as if he had the right to dictate such things. "You could probably live indefinitely on the proceeds, if you were careful."

Savannah could feel a tiny muscle twitching under

her right eye. "And do what?" she hissed. She'd go crazy, just sitting around some parlor, waiting to get old and die.

"Something worthwhile," Parrish answered, undaunted. His tone was mild. Reasonable. Damnably certain. "Like nursing. You handled yourself fairly well with the Leebrook girl. You might even have a talent in that direction."

Nursing? Who would accept care from her, a saloon woman and supposed prostitute? No one, that's who. "Thank you," she said evenly, "for the benefit of your wisdom."

He grinned and raised an invisible glass in an impudent toast. "At your service," he said.

CHAPTER

～≈ 5 ≈～

THE ENCOUNTER at the Brimstone Saloon set the tone for other meetings, in the days and nights to follow, or so it seemed to Savannah. A sort of prickly tolerance arose between her and the doctor, both of them going on about their business, each giving the other as wide a berth as possible. It wasn't always easy, this last, given the crowded state of the Springwater station, and the fact that both of them were staying there.

Savannah had been "in town," as Jacob and Junebug McCaffrey so optimistically said, for nearly a month when Rachel and Trey's mail-order house arrived from Seattle, over a period of three sultry midsummer days, via a variety of freight wagons. Each new arrival was an occasion of much excitement and speculation, and on the fourth day, as if by magic, people began arriving from far-flung farms and ranches, the men armed with tools and opinions, no doubt, the women with preserves and quilt pieces to be shared or exchanged.

Savannah watched the gathering of friendly females from a distance, and with no little envy, learning from Emma that this one was Evangeline Wainwright, wife of Scully, a prosperous rancher, that one was Mrs. Bellweather, mother of Kathleen, who attended school at Springwater, and there was Granny Johnson, who was looking sprightly despite her ailment. June-bug had visited the old woman often over the past few weeks, Savannah knew, and so had Dr. Parrish.

Not, of course, that Savannah had been paying overmuch attention to what Dr. Parrish did. She couldn't help noticing, though, that he didn't drink or gamble when he came to the Brimstone Saloon, though he often took a chair at this table or that, listening earnestly to the tales of drovers, peddlers, and just-plain drifters passing through. More than once, she saw him mount one of Jacob's horses and set out with harried, grim-faced riders, sent by some trail boss to fetch him. Cowboys being cowboys, the doctor was in high demand for setting broken bones, treating snake-bite, and digging out the odd bullet. He continued to pass his nights in the McCaffrey hayloft, insofar as Savannah knew, and took his meals with good appetite, according to June-bug's unbidden reports.

Now, with the sparse though enthusiastic populace of the region clustered in the high grass next to Trey and Rachel's home site, he materialized again, pushing up his sleeves with the rest of them.

Now, the steady *thwack-thwack* of hammers rang up and down the rutted road, punctuated by the back-and-forth rasp of saws. Looking on from the front window of the deserted Brimstone Saloon—even the clientele had gone to help raise the walls of the Hargreaves house— Savannah knew a piercing sense of separation and loneliness.

"You ought to go down to the station and join in," Emma said, looking up at her. The child wasn't supposed to be in the saloon, per Rachel's explicit orders, but she must have had the run of it before her father's marriage the year before, because she knew every inch of the place—where everything was kept, what brands of whiskey were to be had, the rules of every game of chance.

Savannah gave a slight snort and looked down at her bright green silk dress with its resplendence of feathers, bangles, ribbons, and beads. She looked like a tropical bird, or a piece of tasteless furniture run amok. "I don't think I'd fit in very well," she said, in a deliberately pleasant voice, because she liked Emma and already feared that her ungracious response might have offended the child. "Do you?"

Emma shrugged. Her eyes were thoughtful as she turned her gaze to the window again, and the scene beyond, and it came to Savannah that the girl, being half Lakota Sioux, surely knew all about being a misfit. "Pa says everybody who comes out here to the back of beyond has at least one secret, or something that makes them different anyway. That gives us things to learn about each other."

Savannah smiled, albeit a bit sadly. She'd been shunned enough times in her life to know those Springwater women, with their noisy, chasing children, their calico dresses, and baskets full of homey food, would never welcome her into their midst. Miranda, on the other hand, was already one of them, despite her own fall from grace. She'd been helping June-bug cut and assemble quilt pieces for weeks, and it was no secret that she'd developed an eye for Landry Kildare, a handsome rancher with two hellion sons.

"You go ahead," Savannah said to Emma, very gently. "I have things to do here."

Emma took in the empty room. Even the bartender had gone to join in the work party. "What?" she asked reasonably, looking around, as though expecting some task with Savannah's name on it to step up and present itself.

Savannah sighed, laid a hand on Emma's shoulder. "When you're older, you'll understand," she said.

Emma's gaze was narrowed with an intensity of thought. "I think I understand right now," she said. "You've already made up your mind that those women won't like you. You aren't even going to try to be their friend, I'll bet, just because you're scared."

Savannah wondered when this kid had turned into an old woman.

"I'm not scared," she lied.

Emma did not look convinced, to say the least. In fact, she all but rolled her eyes. "You'll be missed, you know," she informed Savannah, shaking a verbal finger under her nose. "Miss June-bug will see you're not there, or Rachel will, and they'll come after you, one or the other of them. Maybe both. Mrs. Wainwright, too, probably. She's real sociable."

Savannah was still dealing with Emma's insights, and the prospect of being sought out and dragged into the center of the festivities was more troubling than being deliberately excluded. Emma was, after all, a bright, damnably observant child, and she didn't miss the fact that Savannah was flustered.

"You're scared," the girl accused baldly, and for the second time.

Savannah's heart did a half-turn, then tightened. She swallowed. No sense in lying; this child would see through any attempt at subterfuge. "Scared isn't exactly the word."

"Oh, yes it is," Emma replied. In that instant, she looked more like her father, who could be downright implacable when the spirit moved him, than ever.

"I agree," put in a masculine voice, from just inside the swinging doors. Prescott Parrish, of course; the man was a plague, or so she constantly told herself. She would have done anything to be able to change the way she reacted to his presence, but she'd long since learned that there was no changing it. Every time he came into a room, especially unexpectedly, her heart started thrumming, and pretty soon all her pulses were beating like drums. "You're a coward, Miss Rigbey," he observed. "You'd tuck your fancy feathers and crawl under the floorboards if you could."

Savannah's gaze shot to the doctor's face. Who did he think he was, coming into her place of business, saying things like that? Making things tighten and melt inside her? "How kind of you to come all this way," she said sweetly, "just to share your opinion."

Emma looked from one adult to the other and, being no fool, made a hasty excuse, turned tail, and fled.

Parrish favored Savannah with one of his lopsided, lord-of-the-manor grins. He looked good, damn him, brown from the sun, his formerly gaunt frame filled out from June-bug's fine cooking. His eyes strayed along the length of her before coming back to lock with her blue ones; the impact was equivalent to a pair of railroad cars coupling on a spur. "I wish I could take the credit," he said. "For affronting you with my opinion, I mean." He shrugged, and his mouth took on a mock-rueful shape. "As it happens, though, I'm merely an emissary for Mrs. McCaffrey. Your absence from the festivities has been noted and commented upon. A decree has gone out, from June-bug if not Caesar Augustus, that you are to present yourself at the station forthwith, there to sew, cook, or just gossip with the other females of the community. It looks as though this house-building party might go on for days."

Savannah felt such a yearning that she feared it showed in her eyes; her pride, usually a fortress in which she could take refuge, teetered around her, providing only the most tenuous shelter. "You ought to know, if June-bug doesn't, why I have to stay away."

Parrish raised an eyebrow. His arms remained folded, and after letting her squirm for a few moments, he repeated his earlier accusation. "Coward," he said.

Savannah realized that she'd clenched her hands into fists, fists full of green beaded silk, and forced her fingers to go slack. "Look at me," she responded, with a note of desperation in her voice. "In case you haven't noticed, I'm not wearing calico."

He ran his eyes over her again. "Oh, I've noticed," he said dryly. "God help me, I *have* noticed."

"Tell June-bug that I'm—I'm busy."

"She's not stupid, Savannah. She'll just come down here after you yourself, even if it means endangering her immortal soul by setting foot inside a den of iniquity like the Brimstone Saloon."

Savannah feared that he was right. She looked out the window again, too miserable even to clasp at the last tattered shreds of her dignity. She'd faced outlaws in her time, as well as drunken, marauding cowboys and miners and Pony Express men too long on the trail. None of them had unnerved her the way those ordinary women did, in their blessedly plain dresses. Only when the doctor took a gentle hold on her arm and turned her to face him did she realize she was gnawing on her lower lip.

Parrish laid a hand to her cheek, passed the pad of his thumb lightly over her mouth, as if to smooth away the evidence of her distress. She should have pulled away from him right then, she knew that, but she didn't. There were so many things she should have done, and hadn't.

"Under all that rouge and kohl and rice powder," he said quietly, "you are more than passably pretty. Even if you were ugly as dried mud, you'd still have as much right to participate as any of the others."

Savannah's heart did something acrobatic, something she hoped to high heaven hadn't shown in her face. "I believe there is a compliment hidden away in that insult," she said, and could not help the shaky smile that came to her mouth.

He laughed, but he did not lower his hand. "Tact has never been my strong suit," he said. "Come on, Savannah. Join the party, or June-bug, for one, won't get a moment's joy out of it, for fretting about you. I suppose you've noticed that social events are not exactly thick on the ground here at Springwater."

She let out a long, despairing sigh. "How can I go in these clothes?"

"I'll head back to the station and fetch whatever you need. You have a few—" he chose the word carefully, *"proper* things. I've seen you wear them. I assume whatever underthings you have on will suffice?" From the look in his eyes, she guessed that he was thinking she must not be wearing any, given the revealing nature of her dance-hall getup. The hell of it was, he was right, though she sure wasn't about to say so.

Savannah knew she was beaten; June-bug, kind hearted to a fault, would indeed come looking for any lost sheep, and if she still refused to attend the festivities, her friend was sure to fret over the fact, thereby missing out on all the fun herself. "The blue skirt, then. And the white shirtwaist. They're on pegs, in my room."

Parrish executed an abbreviated salute. "Back in a trice," he said, and was gone. Savannah watched, through the window, as he strode off down the road again, strong arms swinging at his sides. It seemed that he'd made a place for himself at Springwater, for all his faults and foibles, and she envied him that. She also missed the feel of his hand resting against her cheek, missed the stroke of his thumb and the warm pressure of those nimble surgeon's fingers, though she would have been even less willing to admit to it than to confess that she coveted his ease of belonging.

As promised, he returned in good time, with her clothes draped over one arm. She did wish he had come by the back way, instead of striding straight down the middle of the road, for all and sundry to see.

"Don't forget to wash your face," he said, in a confidential whisper, plainly drawn toward the buzzing hive of builders at Trey and Rachel's place.

Savannah was almost grateful for that remark, even though it shot through her, stinging like turpentine poured over a fresh cut. She'd best get her schoolgirl feelings toward this man under control. He clearly looked down on her; hadn't he criticized her clothing and her face paint and her occupation time and time again?

"Thank you," she said briskly, almost snatching her good skirt and shirtwaist from his arms.

He gave her high marks for courage, but then he'd known that about her almost from the first. Even back in Choteau, when he'd watched her working the crowd that frequented the Hell-bent Saloon, he'd noticed how she always kept her backbone straight and her chin up, how she looked people straight in the eye and gave as good as she got in just about every kind of situation.

He would have given a great deal himself, just then, to watch her with the women parlaying around June-bug McCaffrey's long tables. He had no doubt that she could hold her own, and it had surprised him to discover that she didn't share the same confidence. She really was scared, pretty as she looked in her prim little skirt and blouse, with that fine face of hers scrubbed with such vigor that he could see the glow even from a distance. She'd taken her hair down—the thought of that tightened something in his groin—brushed out countless loopy curls, and rearranged the coppery tresses into a loose bun just above her nape.

A good-natured punch in the arm jolted Pres out of his musings; he turned his head and saw Trey Hargreaves standing beside him, grinning with all the pride of a homeowner. "Jacob and me, we've been talking," Hargreaves said. "Looks like there's going to be a fair amount of lumber left over, after we're through here. There's some from when they built the station, too. We—I'm speaking for the town now—we'd like to put up a little place for you, over there behind the Brimstone. Nothing fancy, of course. Just a couple of rooms and a place where you could attend to folks when they have need of a doctor."

Pres was taken aback by the magnitude of the offer. He hadn't considered settling at Springwater, or anywhere else for that matter. He'd gotten stranded there, that was all, and that wasn't the same thing as deciding. "You'd do that?" he asked, amazed.

Trey grinned. "Hell, yes. You'll never get rich, mind.

There isn't a lot of cash money around here, and I don't imagine there'll ever be, unless somebody strikes gold. But we need a doctor, if we're going to make this a place where folks will want to settle down, and all of us pretty much agree that you'd do."

Pres shoved a hand through his hair, somewhat at a loss. He'd been living in the McCaffreys' hayloft—not a cold or uncomfortable place, though certainly a humble one—and he supposed he'd probably worked off the cost of his room and board. Summer wouldn't last forever, however, and even though he'd earned the price of a stagecoach ticket several times over, putting splints and bandages on hapless cowpunchers, most of his patients had paid him in venison, dried beans, fresh eggs, or stewing chickens. He'd kept the money for much-needed supplies, and given the food to June-bug; she and Jacob had a veritable army to feed, what with all those kids, the studious, blossoming Miranda and her baby, himself, and Savannah.

"I guess I don't have anything better to do," he said, at some length.

Trey laughed and slapped him on the shoulder. "Glad to hear it," he said, and then lowered his voice by several notches to confide, "I think my Rachel might be in the family way. She's peevish of late, and queasy in the mornings. I'd sure feel a lot better knowing you were going to be around to catch the baby."

It was a common phrase, "catch the baby," but it always struck Pres as humorous, raising a mental image of an infant shooting through the air like a cannonball, with the attending physician scrambling, arms outspread. He indicated the assemblage of house parts and eager if inept carpenters with a nod of his head. "Looks like you and the missus will have a roof, walls, and floors before a week's out," he said. His mind had returned to Savannah by then; he imagined her living in the soon-to-be vacant rooms over the Brimstone and felt a sense of indignation rise within him like steam.

"Looks like it," Trey agreed. His gaze was at once proud and fond as he glanced toward the walls of the station, behind which the women were huddled, busy as a flock of hens pecking up corn kernels. "Rachel will be glad to see the last of that saloon, and we'll have Emma with us again, too." He paused and shook his head. "I'm in debt up to my ears, though, and that's a fact," he added ruefully.

"I guess Savannah—Miss Rigbey—will go to live in the rooms you and Rachel have been using," Pres said. He imagined amorous cowboys sneaking up the stairs of a night, stray bullets rising through the floor. His belly ground painfully, and his fists clenched and unclenched at his sides, with no conscious instructions from his mind.

Trey's expression was serious all of the sudden, and a little too astute for Pres's comfort. "She's not a whore, you know," he said. "I've been Savannah's friend for a long time now—five years or so. Except for my Rachel, there's no finer woman in the world."

Pres ran his hand over his jaw; his beard was coming in, but then, it was always coming in. He ought to just give up and let it grow, that being the fashion, but he didn't like the feel of hair on his face; it was unhygienic and, furthermore, it itched. "You don't need to explain Miss Rigbey to me," he said, with an implied shrug.

Trey offered no trace of a smile now; his eyes were slightly narrowed, and everything about him testified that he was in earnest. "Don't I?" he asked. "I've seen you watching her, Doc. And since you don't come to the Brimstone to drink or play cards, I figure Savannah must be the reason you spend so much time there."

Pres folded his arms. "Are you about to warn me off, after that friendly speech about how the 'town' needs a doctor and I'll do as well as the next sawbones to wander down the trail?"

"No," Trey said, still solemn. "I can see that there's something between the two of you, everybody can—except for you and her, maybe. What I'm telling you is this: Savannah's a friend of mine. One of the best I've ever had. I'm prepared to like you—fact is, I already do—but if you treat my partner as anything short of a lady, I'll leave you with some marks to show for your mistake."

Pres had never run from a fight in his life—unless, of course, you counted the ones he might have had with himself—and he wasn't about to start then. Still, he had wondered about Savannah, through many a long night.

"What happened to her?" he asked.

Trey raised his hat and thrust a hand through his hair. "I'm not sure. Something pretty bad, I reckon. She's got no family that I know of, and before she came here, I'm pretty sure I was the only friend she had. If you want to know what makes Savannah who she is, Doc, you ought to ask her." The hint of a grin might have been lurking at the back of his mercury-colored eyes; Pres couldn't be sure.

"She's as likely to spit in my eye as answer," he said.

Trey laughed. "You're right about that," he agreed, as Jacob approached.

He still looked surprised that the house had arrived, since he'd oft predicted that it wouldn't get there before spring. He kept glancing back and shaking his head.

"I'll be derned," he said, for the hundredth time.

Pres slapped him on the back. "Life is full of surprises," he said, and then wondered if he wasn't addressing himself as well as Jacob.

Jacob McCaffrey was nothing if not a good sport. Voice booming, brooding eyes full of good-natured understanding, he demanded, "You two mean to stand around here jawin' and leave the rest of us to do the real work?"

Trey and Pres exchanged another look, then went their separate ways, Trey to help assemble the roof, Pres to unload lumber and kegs of nails alongside Landry Kildare.

They all looked up when Savannah entered the public room of the station, as though sensing that there was an imposter in their midst. June-bug beamed at her, and Rachel's expression was friendly, too, but the others were watchful, assessing the newcomer and being none too subtle in the process. Had they been discussing her before her arrival? Just the thought made Savannah want to run until her knees gave out—to hell with Dr. Parrish and his chiding and his challenges.

Rachel brought an attractive, fair-haired woman over to her, almost shyly. "Savannah," she said, "this is my dearest friend in all the world, Evangeline Wainwright. We knew each other in Pennsylvania. Evangeline, Savannah Rigbey. She's an—investor."

Without hesitation, Evangeline put out a strong, slender hand. "I'm very pleased to meet you," she said, in a clear voice. She was smiling warmly, and her eyes were full of light. "Will you be settling here at Spring-water?"

Savannah stammered something, though her mind was whirling at such a pace that she didn't know what. An *investor?*, she thought. What could have prompted Rachel to assign her such a title? Everyone would know—must already know—that she owned half inter-est in the Brimstone Saloon, that she worked there, sang there, sold whiskey there. But then, those things probably couldn't even be *mentioned* in polite company. "Yes," she answered belatedly. Weakly. "I'm staying."

"Come and sit down," Rachel said, pulling her toward the tables, where the women had laid out a series of colorful quilt pieces, apparently working out a pattern. "June-bug's made tea, and there's coffee, too, if you'd rather have that. What do you think of the wedding ring?"

"Wedding ring?" Savannah echoed stupidly. She might have been wearing regular clothes, but she felt as if she were still in silk and feathers. The paint, washed off because it was only sensible and certainly not because Dr. Parrish had suggested that she do so, left a sort of physical echo on her face.

Evangeline laughed, but pleasantly, the way she probably laughed with Rachel and the others. Savannah was heartily confused, having been scorned so many times in the past, by just such women as these.

"It's the name of a quilt pattern," Evangeline said. "See?" She pointed out the interlocking circles of colored fabric worked into the squares.

Savannah's hand trembled slightly, but she couldn't stop herself from reaching out, touching the cloth. She'd always dreamed of owning such a quilt; to her, the colorful patterns symbolized normalcy. "How beautiful," she said, and blinked rapidly, fearing she would disgrace herself and weep for all she had missed.

After working up her nerve, she looked from one face to another, and it seemed to her that the women were not so wary, nor so severe, as when she'd first come in. Those she didn't know were still a little distant, though. "Did you all contribute?"

One woman—Savannah would later know her as Mrs. Bellweather—spared a nod. Miranda, seated at the far end of the table with a pile of bright scraps before her, was watching Savannah with an expression of eager encouragement in her eyes, like someone trying to persuade a baby to take its first faltering steps.

"It's for the next Springwater bride," Evangeline said, eyes bright. "We made one for Rachel already—

Jacob's ladder, it's called—and mine is a log cabin pattern. June-bug and Sue stitched that one up, over a snowy winter."

Savannah looked about. Her throat felt tight. "Someone is about to be married?"

Rachel laughed. "No one in particular. We're all sewing our bits and pieces of calico together, though, and matching them up when we meet. When there's a wedding, we'll be ready."

Savannah was charmed and a little bemused. She sat down, at only a slight distance from the others, on one of the long benches, and June-bug set a steaming cup of tea in front of her, already laced with milk and sugar, just the way she liked it. "She'll be a lucky bride, whoever she is," Savannah said, perhaps a bit wistfully.

"I hope it's someone for Landry," said another woman, the wife of a farmer. "Poor man. All alone, with those demon boys of his to raise. Mark my words, one of these nights, they'll burn the house down, with him right inside."

Miranda, who had been sewing industriously again, seemed to catch on Kildare's name like a fish on a hook. "How does it happen that he's got no wife?" she asked shyly. "Somebody as fine to look at as he is, I mean."

The others giggled, though not unkindly, but Miranda went brick-red all the same. Savannah felt sorry for her, though she hadn't been able to help smiling a little herself. Just for a very few moments, she forgot that she could never truly be a member of this little group; she was, after all, a dance-hall woman and assumed prostitute. If it hadn't been for June-bug and perhaps Rachel, the others probably wouldn't have spoken to her at all.

"Well," insisted Evangeline, seated across from Savannah, beside her good friend Rachel, and stitching away, "he *is* handsome. Landry, I mean."

"Had him a wife once," said another woman, after everyone had clucked over Evangeline's daring remark. "The cholera took her. Pretty thing, delicatelike, with quiet ways."

Miranda twisted her hands, her face a study in sympathy for all the Kildares. "It's a terrible thing, the cholera," she said. "We saw plenty of it on the way out here from St. Louis." She paused. "How long ago was that? When Mrs. Kildare passed over, I mean?"

"Must have been quite a while back," June-bug put in. "It was before Jacob and I came to run the station. He already had that place of his when we got here."

"He was one of the first to settle around here," affirmed Mrs. Bellweather, who looked worn-down to Savannah, as though she'd known too much hardship, too much work and sorrow for one body to sort through. "Came to this country about the same time as Big John Keating and Scully Wainwright." She paused and tightened her narrow little mouth. "She's buried right there, too. They say he used to sleep beside that grave, till the weather got too cold."

Rachel and Evangeline exchanged glances and stitched a little faster.

"What was her name?" Miranda dared to ask. Her

voice was hardly more than a whisper, and her fingers were knotted together, white at the knuckles, her quilt square forgotten on the table before her.

"Caroline," the woman answered, after a few moments of consideration. "Why do you ask?"

Miranda flushed and swallowed.

June-bug laid an affectionate hand to the girl's shoulder. "She's just curious, that's all," she said, with a broad smile, neatly dismissing the subject. "Nothin' wrong with that."

The sewing continued, and so did the talk, the pouring and sipping of tea, the merry laughter. Savannah was glad she'd locked up the saloon and ventured into this circle of women; maybe they hadn't exactly enfolded her, but they hadn't shut her out, either. She was a part of the group, if only at the fringes, and she relished the novelty of that, pretending to herself, just for that long, hot afternoon, that she was an ordinary wife, with a house to keep, and a husband to feed and humor and plague about flower seeds and glass windows and what to make for supper.

The preparation of the evening meal was a spectacular enterprise, with tasks for everyone to perform, all of them orchestrated by June-bug, and Savannah was included without hesitation. Although she knew little or nothing about cooking, she did remember how to peel potatoes, so June-bug assigned her that job.

Now and then, one or another of the men straggled in, looking for coffee and a temporary place out of the sun, but they soon became uncomfortable in the presence of so many women and departed again. Until

Dr. Parrish came in, that is. He stood quietly on the hearth, leaning at his ease against the mantelpiece, cup in hand. His ebony eyes sought Savannah, found her, held her captive, by means of some strange and elemental magic. She did not look at him directly—refused to do so—but she was aware of his observance all the same, conscious of him in every cell of her body and every wisp of her soul.

She was annoyed to find herself in such a state, again. She wanted to run, from him, from the calm embrace of Springwater itself, to get up from that table, throw her few belongings into a satchel, and dash off into the night, without even bothering to choose a direction first. She could not, would not ever be vulnerable again; the one time she had let down her guard, she'd all but ruined her life.

Unconsciously, she raised a hand to her mouth in abject panic, realized what she'd revealed only when it was too late. When he'd seen, of course, and understood. The expression in his eyes said he understood only too well.

She managed a smile as she stood, on unsteady legs, the room seeming, for the merest fraction of a moment, to sway and dip around her. It was ridiculous to react in such a fashion. Downright silly. She was not a schoolgirl, for heaven's sake, not some witless virgin, far from home, but an accomplished business woman, a person of substance and common sense. She should know better, be able to control her responses, even to quell them entirely, when that would be suitable.

"Good night," she said, to the general assembly, and

turned, very nearly stumbling over her own feet, to make a beeline for the door.

Outside, on the step, she drew in great, gulping draughts of fresh evening air, hugging herself with both arms against the chill. Across the road, the men were still working, their shirts soaked through with sweat. The framework of Trey and Rachel's house was already outlined against the dusky sky, where the first stars were just beginning to pop out.

"Are you all right?"

She should have been prepared for him to follow her, should have expected it, but she hadn't. "No," she said, without turning to look at him. "No," she repeated.

He came to stand beside her, his upper arm brushing, just barely, against her shoulder, sending a shock of sensation bolting through her. "Perhaps you should go in and lie down." He looked and sounded genuinely concerned.

She shook her head. "I'll be fine in a minute or two." She pressed the fingertips of her right hand to her temple. "They spoke to me. They're planning a quilt, to present to the next bride. They don't even know who it will be—" She was rambling, prattling, could not seem to stop herself, or even slow her tongue.

Suddenly, he took hold of her, turned her to face him, and lowered his mouth to hers. The kiss was fiery, consuming, and desperate, and might have led to all manner of troubles, had it not raised a rousing cheer from the other side of the road.

CHAPTER

6

THOUGH THERE WAS still a lot of finishing work to do on the Hargreaves house, outside as well as in, the place was habitable after only a week of concentrated community effort. There was a working wood furnace to provide heat when the fierce Montana winters came, and glass in the windows. The fancy plumbing and other luxuries would take longer to install, and the pre-cut wooden floors were bare of varnish, let alone rugs. The fireplace in the front parlor consisted of a pile of rocks gathered from the countryside and a few bags of dry mortar, but the small family did not seem to mind the prospect of rough accommodations. With appropriate ceremony, Trey, Rachel, and the child Emma took up residence, hurrahed by their friends and presented with gifts—food, mostly, every sort of preserved vegetable, fruit, and meat, but firewood, too, and what spare linens could be ferreted from trunks and bureaus. Jacob McCaffrey was already building a cradle out in the barn behind the station; Pres was the only one who knew, that being unavoidable since he was still sleeping in the hayloft then.

It made an ache in him, the sight of that cradle; for the first time in years, he wanted children of his own. And he wanted them by Savannah. Exasperating as she was, even impossible at times, she'd taken up residence in all his senses at once, infused his mind and his spirit with her own, until he couldn't tell one from the other. Was this love?

God in heaven, he hoped not.

In the meantime, the promised house/surgery was well under way, utilizing the modest surplus of supplies remaining after the Hargreaves' place had been pieced together, like the parts of a giant puzzle, though most of the work was being done by Trey, Jacob, and Pres himself, with an occasional helping hand from Landry. The others had had to leave for home, since all of them had farms and ranches to run; most left reluctantly in the charge of son, brother, or hired hand.

Savannah had not yet moved in above the saloon— June-bug was vociferously opposed to that, bless her— and besides, she didn't appear to own a stick of furniture, so she remained at the station, in the little room behind the kitchen stove.

As the days began to grow shorter, ever so slowly, and colder as well, Pres wished he could share it with her. Thoughts of Savannah and babies and patchwork quilts disturbed his sleep and distracted him during his waking hours.

Finally, the last week in August, when a series of

heavy rains came, turning the fields to a dense mud the locals called "gumbo"—Jacob allowed as how it wasn't uncommon for the weather to turn suddenlike and counted them all blessed of the Lord—Pres was able to move into his own humble dwelling. He soon found that the place was only a little warmer than the McCaffrey barn had been, but at least there was a rusty old stove, scavenged from an abandoned homestead a few miles from town. He had a bed, hastily nailed together by Jacob, with rope to support the mattress June-bug and Miranda stitched together from flour sacks and last year's corn husks, and a table, fashioned from one of the crates in which the Hargreaves' mail-order mansion had arrived. His chairs were of similar construction, and the floor was so poorly planed that he didn't dare set his feet down in the morning without pulling on his boots first. Come winter, there would probably be a layer of frost to greet him as well.

In spite of all these shortcomings, Pres was happier than he had been in a long time. There was no lack of patients from the first day, and every passing stagecoach brought more of the supplies and medicines he'd sent to Choteau for. He took his meals at the station, having no pots, dishes, or skill for cooking, though of course his reasons had more to do with Savannah than with June-bug McCaffrey's victuals. Now that he was practicing medicine again, he simply didn't have the leisure to pass long hours at the Brimstone, pretending not to watch her.

It was ill advised, he knew, this fascination with a woman who obviously mistrusted him. Ever since that night when she'd taken her rightful place among the ladies of Springwater, and he'd been brash enough to kiss her in front of half the population on the front step shortly afterward, she'd been keeping a careful distance. Not that he'd apologize or anything, given that he'd meant to do it, all right, and wouldn't do differently even if he could go back to that night and take another run at the whole encounter.

He was considering the matter of Savannah Rigbey, between advising June-bug McCaffrey on her arthritis and an aging cowboy on his dyspepsia, when all of the sudden the surgery door blew open and Savannah herself swept in with a rainy wind, wrapped in a brown velvet cloak with a graceful hood. Great droplets of water clung to her lashes and her clothes, but her eyes were fiery enough to dry up a lake.

"Shut the door," Pres said reasonably.

"Dr. Parrish—"

"Prescott," he corrected her, lifting his donated coffeepot from the top of the little stove and giving it a shake to see if anything remained of the batch he'd made at breakfast. "Pres, if you want to be friendly. Tell me, where does it hurt?"

She slammed the door. "I *don't* want to be friendly, as it happens," she snapped, "and nothing hurts."

He enjoyed watching her temper flare almost as much as kissing her. "Then to what do I owe the honor of this visit?"

"I think it would be better for everyone if you just left town," she announced. She'd folded her arms, and under the hem of her dress he saw that one small foot was tapping soundlessly against the splintery floor, though whether from nerves or temper, he couldn't tell. "Move on, I mean. From Springwater."

The surgery, like the sleeping quarters to the rear, was scantly furnished. "Sit down," he said, indicating one of the packing-crate chairs with a cordial nod. Then he lifted the dented pot. "Coffee?"

She sat, but not graciously. Nor did she take off her cloak. Under the table, he suspected, that same foot was still tapping. She was acting as though she were angry, but her eyes conveyed something else—a sort of despairing confusion. "Did you hear what I said?"

He grinned, pouring a dose of what could only be described as axle grease for himself. "Oh, yes," he said. "My hearing is fairly good, actually, despite three and a half years of almost constant canon fire. Why do you want me to leave?"

She looked very uncomfortable and a little peevish. Barely eleven A.M., by his father's pocket watch, and already the day was shaping up to be a memorable one. "Because—" she hesitated, visibly searching for words. She had not thought this visit through beforehand, it would seem, but instead come on impulse. "Because you kissed me. Twice."

He kept his distance, lest he scare her away. "Is there an ordinance against that?" he asked, very cheerfully.

He was rewarded by the apricot blush that rose in her cheeks. God in heaven, but she was breathtaking. Body, mind, spirit, he loved—yes, loved—everything about her.

Savannah laid both hands on the tabletop, palms down, with a little slapping sound. She took several slow, deep breaths, and closed her eyes for a moment, in an admirable bid for control. "I would leave myself," she said moderately, and at some length, "but I've tied up every penny I have in that dratted saloon."

"Maybe Trey Hargreaves would be willing to buy you out. If you really want to move on, I mean." It was a bluff; the last thing he wanted was for her to go anywhere. She was, of course, the reason he'd stayed on at Springwater in the first place, though he'd be a pure fool to say as much, under the circumstances.

She leaned forward a little way, providing a tantalizing glimpse of cleavage despite her heavy cloak, and gave him that look he'd seen her use to intimidate obnoxious cowboys. It wasn't going to work with him.

"It would be much easier," she said reasonably, "if *you* were the one to leave."

"Why is that?"

"Because there's nothing holding you here, really. Except for this—this shack."

"And my patients," he added. He was doing his best not to smile, since he figured that might prompt her to get up and walk out, but it wasn't easy. Even—maybe *especially*—in a state of agitation, she was a pleasure to watch and a balm to his jaded spirit. "Mustn't forget them. And you still haven't answered my question, Miss Rigbey. Not really."

She looked at him in stubborn silence, though she knew damn well what he meant.

All right, he'd give in. "Why do you want me to leave? Besides as a punishment for daring to kiss you, I mean?"

She bit down hard on that luscious lower lip of hers. He wanted to nibble at it, along with a few other sensitive parts of her anatomy. Her eyes got very wide and darkened a little, and that delectable peachy color pulsed beneath her cheekbones again. "You're going to make me say it, aren't you?"

"Yes," he said bluntly. He allowed himself just the suggestion of a grin and waited, arms folded again, coffee mug forgotten on the nearby windowsill.

"I can't think. I can't sleep." Her color heightened still further, and she seemed to have trouble meeting his eyes. There was a note of desperation in her voice. "I can't afford to fall—to feel—"

He crossed to her then, dragged up the other chair to sit facing her, and leaned in a little, his nose an inch from hers. "To fall where, Miss Rigbey? And feel what?"

To his utter surprise, and his chagrin, sudden tears welled in her eyes. She raised her chin a notch, just the same. "I was in love once, or I thought so, anyway," she said, and if she'd refused to look at him before, now she wouldn't look away. "His name was Burke—I knew him, growing up. He was already wild, even as a boy, but after we ran off, well, he—he—"

He tightened his grip on her hands, spoke quietly. "What, Savannah?"

"We were about to get married." Her smile was wobbly and fragile. "The fact is, we were standing before the justice of the peace. A U.S. Marshal interrupted the ceremony to arrest Burke. Turned out, he'd been involved in some robberies. They took him away, then and there, and later on, he was convicted and sent to prison."

Pres ached for her, for the woman before him, and for the young girl she had been. "What did you do?"

She looked at him with round, fearful eyes, as though expecting judgment. "I went home," she said. "Papa called me a whore and told me never to come back." He ached to pull her into his arms, hold her close, but it wasn't time for offering comfort, not yet. She wasn't finished. "I didn't know any other way to earn a living than singing in a saloon. Nobody was going to take me on to watch their children or clean their house, not with the scandal I'd raised. Why, it was even in the newspapers, how I'd eloped with a thief— how Burke was arrested right in the middle of our wedding."

Pres opened his mouth, closed it again. He rasped an exclamation.

Her gaze remained direct, though her pain was as intense as any he'd seen on the battlefields of Pennsylvania, Virginia, Tennessee, and too many other places. He wanted to take her by the shoulders, but she still seemed delicate as glass, ready to shatter at the gentlest touch. "I was only sixteen. I couldn't go to Burke, and there was no one else. So I went to work to support myself."

"There's no shame in that, Savannah. You made a mistake. Welcome to the human race."

She looked at him with mild surprise. "Nevertheless, I've had to live with the consequences. My life was changed forever. And my grandmother died because of what happened."

He frowned. "How do you figure that? Grandmothers die, Savannah."

"She was heartbroken after Papa sent me away. She went into a decline. Papa made sure I heard about it, and when I tried to go to her funeral, he had me barred from the church."

Pres wanted to overturn tables and fling things in every direction, a feeling he'd had many times during the war, though he had never indulged himself and didn't intend to begin now. "Your father was wrong, Savannah. And you're wrong, too, if you blame yourself. What you did wasn't evil, or malicious. It was natural for a young girl, believing herself to be in love. Does it make sense to spend the rest of your life under your father's wrongheaded judgment?"

She blinked, obviously jarred by the question, and said nothing.

"Savannah," he persisted, but gently. If she fled him now, he knew, she would never come back.

She ran her tongue over her lips; it was merely a

nervous reaction, nothing more, and yet it set his groin to aching. "I was an ordinary girl," she said, "with a good singing voice, a head for numbers, and a whole passel of dreams I was sure would come true. I had a grandmother and a father who loved me—once—and friends. Lots and lots of friends. I wanted to have children, six of them, and head up the church choir. I wanted to cook and go to quilting bees, like Gran did—"

He waited, even when her voice fell away.

"Two months after my grandmother died, Papa passed away, too. Up until then, I could pretend that things might be all right again, that he might forgive me. Once he was gone, though, I had to accept the fact that I was probably going to spend the rest of my life in saloons. In some ways, that was the worst moment of all."

"It must have been a lot like my first shift in a field hospital. Nothing I learned in medical college prepared me for what I found in that place."

A long silence fell between them, oddly comfortable, given the situation and the topic of conversation.

"Was it very terrible?" She barely breathed the words.

"Beyond that," he answered, and sighed, letting her hands go, resting his palms on his knees. They were still facing each other, still very close. "I don't suppose I'll ever completely leave it behind. But I'm trying, Savannah. That's the point. You've got to do the same. We need to shake off these demons of ours, both of us."

He saw a protest forming on her mouth, in her eyes,

but in the end she did not offer it. "I'm not sure I can do it," she whispered. It was a momentous admission for her; he could see that.

He had never wanted to kiss her as much as he did in that moment, and that was saying something, considering how much time he'd spent lying in Jacob McCaffrey's hayloft, staring up at the log beams and aching to do just that and a whole lot more. He restrained himself, and what he said astonished him as much as it did Savannah. "Marry me."

She stared at him, and her mouth dropped open—he put one hand under her chin and lifted, closing her jaw. "You're not serious," she said, in the next moment.

"I think I am," he said. He'd given the idea a lot of consideration, all the while trying to fool himself into believing that it was only idle speculation. Now, it seemed as if he'd glanced inside himself one day, while passing by, and found another person there, someone better than he'd been until he came to Springwater, someone capable of loving and believing and hoping that the future could be better than the past.

"But why?"

He wasn't ready to tell her how he felt. He was still explaining it to himself. "Because you need a husband and I need a wife. Plenty of people have gotten married for less practical reasons."

"You're insane!" She flushed yet again, and her hands rose to her hips, though she looked more broken than angry. "We're not in love—"

"Be sensible, Savannah," he counseled, as if he was

being sensible himself. "You're not happy running the Brimstone Saloon and wearing those silly dresses—admit that to yourself, if not to me. You were a great help when Miranda's baby came—calm and competent. You'd make a fine nurse and a very good doctor's wife."

"You'd marry someone who's spent most of her life singing to drunken cowboys?"

"Yes," he answered. Savannah was levelheaded, for the most part, and she had an unruffled, caring way about her. He'd liked the way she'd spoken soothingly to Miranda, during the height of the girl's labor, the way she'd held the baby almost reverently, not caring that the squirming, squalling little creature hadn't been washed or wrapped. She could be firm, too, obviously, when the situation called for it.

She got up, and for a moment he feared she meant to leave, but instead she began to pace, like a lawyer formulating an impassioned appeal to put before a waiting jury. "Where would I sleep?" she asked.

The question caught him so off guard that he nearly swallowed his tongue. "With me," he replied, at some length, and in a voice he nearly didn't recognize.

She stopped, and her eyes were wide again. "You mean—?"

"That's exactly what I mean," he clarified. "A wife is a wife. I expect mine to share my bed." No sense having any misunderstandings on that score.

"I am not a whore, Dr. Parrish. I don't sell myself for money, and I won't take a wedding ring for payment either."

He wanted to shake her. Why couldn't she let

herself be happy? But he knew, of course. She was afraid of being hurt, not just physically, but emotionally, too. "I didn't say you were. I said if you marry me, you'll have to lie beside me every night. That's what wives do, among other things." He stood, went to face her, laid his hands gently on her cheeks. "I swear to God, Savannah, I'm not like him. I won't let you down."

She seemed to want to fly off in every direction, and she was trembling, but he could tell that she was entertaining the prospect of marrying him, that she really did want to wear calico and have babies and be called "Mrs." Somebody. Mrs. Parrish, he thought, would do nicely.

"Nobody within fifty miles will be surprised," he said, in case it made a difference. He forgave himself this inanity on grounds of being in shock.

"What is that supposed to mean?"

"Remember how the men cheered when I kissed you, Savannah?" he countered. He dropped his hands from her face, took a light, supportive hold on her upper arms. "Everyone knows we want each other. Everyone but you and, all right, me too, until very recently."

She looked him over, rather like a farmer's wife inspecting a rooster at the fair, prior to purchase. "Suppose you take to drinking again?"

He raised one hand, as if in an oath. "I won't," he argued, but calmly, placing just the merest emphasis on the second word. "I didn't drink before I went into the Army, or during my term of service. It started afterward, Savannah, when I had to stand still long enough for all of it to catch up with me."

She bit her lower lip again and furrowed her brow, afraid to believe in happy endings. He didn't blame her. "Suppose I came to care for you very deeply, and you never returned the sentiment? Suppose you took a mistress—"

"The best kind of love isn't spontaneous, Savannah," he said, wondering where the declaration had come from even as he uttered it. "It grows, over time, because two people live and work together. Because they share a life."

She folded her arms. She was weakening, he could tell. "And the mistress?"

"I wouldn't have the time, let alone the inclination. You have my permission to shoot me if I ever break our vows."

"Don't worry," she said decisively, "I would. With or without your permission."

He grinned. "Then it's settled. When's the wedding?"

She gulped. "It isn't settled. Not at all."

He kissed her then, tenderly at first, teasing her lips apart, then with a passion that, like Paul's experience on the road to Damascus, might just leave him blind for three days. Or so it seemed at the time.

Savannah gasped when he finally withdrew, but she didn't pull out of his arms; indeed, she leaned against him, breathing deeply, letting her forehead rest against his shoulder. "I wouldn't be the sort of wife who takes orders," she warned, after a few moments. "I won't carry your slippers, like a pet spaniel, and if women *ever* get the vote, I'll cast my ballot for whatever candidate I choose. I won't necessarily hold the same opinions as you do. And if I sell my share of the Brimstone to Trey, it might be a very long time before I see a penny of the money. When I do, I intend to bank it in Great Falls or Denver or even San Francisco, under my name and my name alone."

He laughed. "Fine," he said. "I don't mind supporting you. Just be forewarned—country doctors don't make much money, so we won't be living in grand style."

Her eyes were alight with the desire to trust him, to step out of the fortress she'd erected around herself. "I need time to think," she said.

He was jubilant that she hadn't turned him down out of hand. "Do all the thinking you want," he said, but he kissed her again and, again, she didn't resist.

Marriage. To Prescott Parrish.

Was she mad?

The wind was liquid as Savannah walked back toward Springwater station, through a spattering downpour, but she barely noticed. Her senses were a-riot, and it was all Pres's fault for kissing her. For talking about—about the things he'd talked about.

She couldn't actually *marry* the man, of course. Oh, she felt passion for him, even longing. And she'd lived in the world too long not to know that what he'd said about love was true—it didn't always strike unexpectedly, as it had with Rachel and Trey, or the Wain-

wrights. More often, especially between men and
women settling out west, where the work was uncom-
monly hard and there were so many ways to die or be
grievously injured, good marriages began as partner-
ships.

Across the road from the station, lights glowed in the
windows of the Hargreaves' splendid five-room house.
Smoke curled from the chimney over the kitchen
cookstove, and as Savannah stood there, in the gathering rainstorm, she wondered if Trey and Rachel really
knew how lucky they were.

It was then that she decided, or at least, she would
always remember it that way. She would accept Pres's
proposal, and take her chances. Maybe someday, she
might even be able to admit that she loved him, that
she had from the night he'd delivered Miranda's baby.
In the very instant he'd handed her that squalling,
messy newborn child, she'd felt a telling shift, deep
in her soul. She simply hadn't recognized that fierce
and sudden yearning for what it was—how could she
have, when she'd never experienced anything like it
before?

Perhaps, in time, Pres would come to love her in
return.

She went inside the station, found the main room
empty, which was both a relief and a disappointment.
She wanted to tell June-bug her news, and yet she
wasn't quite ready to share it. She hadn't gotten used to
the idea herself, after all, and she would be awhile
working it through.

It was only when she reached her snug little hideaway

behind the cookstove and took off her cloak that she looked down at the scarlet taffeta dress she was wearing and recalled that she'd been headed for the Brimstone when she left the station. In fact, she'd only stopped to call on Dr. Parrish—Pres—on a crazy impulse. He'd kissed her, asked for her hand in marriage, and all the while she'd been wearing the clothes he hated and the "face paint" he'd taken exception to on several occasions.

A door closed in the distance, and she heard June-bug's voice. "Savannah? Darlin', are you sick?" The other woman appeared in the entryway to Savannah's room, wearing a lightweight bonnet and a woolen cloak. Her brow was crumpled in a worried expression. "Weren't you headed to the Brimstone?"

Savannah had no explanation to offer, even to herself, but in that moment, she burst into tears and sat down hard on the edge of her bed. June-bug discarded her bonnet and cloak, cluck-clucking all the while, and came to perch beside her and drape a sympathetic arm around her wobbling shoulders. "Well, sweetheart, what on *earth?*"

"I can't do it anymore!" she wailed.

"Do what?" June-bug asked, reasonably enough.

"Put on these dreadful clothes and all this kohl and rouge and spend all my time in that saloon!" Savannah sobbed.

"There, now," June-bug said, rocking her a little. "There, now." She didn't offer a solution or any sort of advice, and Savannah loved her for those attributes, among many others. "I'll make us some tea. You wash your face and put on another dress. Jacob can step across the way and tell Trey you won't be working tonight."

Savannah had been on her own for a long time, and it was bliss to be mothered for a little while, to be cosseted and comforted and soothed. "Th-that would be n-nice," she snuffled, making a brave effort to collect herself.

June-bug patted Savannah's back before rising to her feet. "Everybody needs a good cry once in a while," she said. "You just carry on all you want."

Savannah couldn't help a small burst of laughter at the advice. "I feel like a perfect fool," she said. "What good does crying do?"

"Why, tears are like medicine," June-bug said, sounding surprised by the question. "They heal all manner of ills and soften up some of our sorrows, too."

Savannah took a pressed handkerchief from the drawer of her bedside table and delicately blew her nose. "My grandmother used to say things like that."

June-bug, poised on the threshold, smiled. "I reckon I would have liked her a lot, your grandmother. Now, you wash your face. You got all them colors to runnin'."

She laughed again, this time with spirit, and when June-bug left the room, she got up, poured water from the pitcher into the washbasin, both items being kept on a scarred table under a high window, and scrubbed her face with one of the few luxuries she allowed herself—fine-milled French soap. Then, when the last streaks of red and blue and black were gone, she let down her hair and brushed it until it crackled. The dress was the last to go—she slipped the garment down over her hips and kicked it over into a corner of the room in a symbolic act. When she joined June-bug for tea, ten minutes later, with her hair in a loose bun at the back of her head, she was wearing a blue bombazine dress, and Jacob had been despatched to deliver the message to Trey.

Her partner came across the road right away, looking worried. "Are you sick?" he asked, in much the same tone as June-bug had done earlier.

Savannah, seated in a rocking chair near the fire, teacup in hand, shook her head in response, unable, for the moment, to explain. June-bug went to look in on Miranda and the baby, still referred to as "little Isaiah-or-Ezekiel," and Jacob herded Toby and Christabel outside to help him with the chores.

Trey drew up the other rocking chair. "What is it, then?"

"I'm going to be married," she said, without planning to. "I don't want to be a saloon-keeper anymore."

From anyone else, she might have expected anger, but Trey was her friend, closer than a brother. She saw immediately that he understood, maybe because he was so happy with Rachel. "Doc Parrish?"

She nodded. So Pres had been right, then. Everyone knew.

Trey beamed. "That's wonderful."

"But our partnership, yours and mine, I mean—"

He was thoughtful. "I can buy you out, if you're willing to wait a spell for the money. A *long* spell, I reckon. If that won't do, we could bring somebody in from Choteau or Great Falls to take your place. Pay them a salary."

Suddenly, Savannah was filled with panic. Suppose she hated being a doctor's wife? Suppose she hated being *Prescott Parrish's* wife? If she sold her share of the saloon to Trey or anyone else, she would have nowhere to turn, nowhere to take refuge.

But that was silly. She could take care of herself, whether penniless or with a fat bank account tucked away in Denver or San Francisco. She had already established that much; she had nothing more to prove, either to herself or to the world in general. Marrying Pres was something she would do simply because it was what she *wanted* to do.

"Savannah?" Trey prompted, and she realized she'd let his suggestion about bringing in someone else to take her place at the saloon go unanswered.

"No," she said firmly, after another moment or two of hard thought. "A marriage can't work, if you've got one foot in the agreement and one foot out, ready to spring for parts unknown. I'll sell, Trey. I know you're a fair man—I wouldn't have dealt with you in the first place if I thought otherwise—so you make me an offer and come up with some terms, and we'll settle the whole thing, once and for all. I don't care how long it takes you to pay me."

Trey's silver eyes were alight, and it gave Savannah something of a pang to realize that he'd probably wanted to own the Brimstone outright for a long time. "I'll have to speak with Rachel, of course," he said, with barely controlled eagerness. "But I think we can consider the sale already made."

Savannah leaned over and kissed her old friend lightly on the forehead. "Thank you, Trey," she told him softly.

No looking back now, she added to herself. It was time to leave all the old demons behind, just as Pres had said, and keep company with angels instead.

CHAPTER

7

THE WEDDING WAS a quiet one, held before the hearth at Springwater station, three days after Pres's unorthodox proposal. Jacob McCaffrey officiated, Trey and Rachel were witnesses, and the children, Emma, Toby, and Christabel, served as eager guests, along with June-bug and the pensive Miranda. Savannah felt wildly dizzy the whole time the brief but binding ceremony was going on, like someone trying to walk blindfolded over uneven ground. By the time it had ended, and Pres had kissed her exuberantly to seal the bargain, she was seeing everything through a haze, and all the ordinary sounds of the room, the station itself, and even the surrounding wilderness were underlaid with a peculiar thrumming buzz.

Pres, ever the doctor, ate cake and accepted congratulations with that strange, blunt grace that, Savannah was learning, was a hallmark of his personality, but his attention had been caught by young Christabel's twisted foot.

"I'd like to have a closer look at that," he confided, with a thoughtful frown creasing his forehead.

Though Savannah was certainly not without sympathy for the shy, crippled child, her mind was fixed on other matters entirely, just then. She was *married*. Someday, with luck and good behavior, she might even be respectable.

And in a very short while, she would be alone with her husband. Sharing the double bed borrowed from Miranda's room at the station; Trey, Jacob, and Pres had dismantled the thing that morning, and carried it over to Pres's "house." Miranda and little Isaiah-or-Ezekiel would move into Savannah's old nook, behind the cookstove. Already, dusk was gathering at the windows, and a light rain had begun to fall, pattering on the roof and against the windows like sweet, rhythmic music. Savannah, who had known the intimate attentions of a man, however unwillingly, who had spent years in the saloon business, was so deliciously nervous that she might have been the most uninitiated of brides.

"Was Christabel born with that bad foot?" Pres asked of Jacob, who was standing nearby, tall and imposing in his dark "preachin' suit." "Or was there an accident?"

"Born with it, I reckon," Jacob said, in his quiet, rumbling way.

June-bug poked Pres in the ribs. He looked wonderfully handsome in the clothes she'd provided, no doubt belonging to one or the other of the lost twins. "Never mind that," she said. "Christabel's foot will keep; she's lived with it this long. This is your *wedding* day, Doc."

A broad grin broke over Pres's handsome face. "Yes," he said, with a sidelong glance at Savannah, who blushed in spite of her best resolve to be circumspect. "It is indeed. I think perhaps it's time for the bride and me to say our farewells, for the night, at least."

Savannah, standing there in her best dress, an ivory silk from her saloon-girl days, hastily altered with bits and pieces from other frocks, judiciously assembled— Savannah, who did not have a retiring bone in her body, lowered her eyes and could not bring herself to raise them again.

She was therefore caught completely by surprise when Pres suddenly swept her up into his arms, right there in the main room of the Springwater station. Everyone applauded merrily, and someone opened the door. A moist breeze rushed in and made the rainy-day fire dance in the grate.

"Put me down," Savannah whispered, though half heartedly, her face buried in Pres's neck.

"Oh, I will," he promised softly, for her ears only. "As soon as we get to our bed." And so it was that he carried her down the middle of the Springwater road, through a misty benediction of rainfall, the skirts of her improvised wedding dress tumbling down over his legs as well as hers. Indeed, he carried her around the back of the Brimstone Saloon and, finally, into the little house/office that would be their home.

The place was chilly, but Savannah didn't feel the low temperature. She was warmed by an inner fire, being held like that, and in such close proximity to

Pres's—her *husband's*—strong chest, wrapped in his arms. He didn't set her down to open their front door, but bent awkwardly, and kicked it closed with the heel of one boot once they'd crossed the threshold. Without so much as pausing, he made for the single room that would be their living quarters for the foreseeable future.

Finally, as promised, he dropped her playfully onto the bed, where she landed in a heap of silk and ruffles and lace, a make-do bride in a make-do wedding dress. His expression was somber as he looked down at her.

"You'll never regret taking me for a husband, Savannah Parrish," he said, and his voice sounded gruff.

Her throat tightened with some emotion it seemed better not to name. "I know that," she replied, and somehow, she *did* know. For all his arrogance, for all his terse tongue and errant past, Pres was a good man, the one the Fates had chosen for her, and presented as a gift. She wanted to say she loved him then, that she'd fallen for him on that first night in Springwater, but she couldn't risk being rebuffed.

He began by undoing his borrowed string tie, loosened his collar, tossed aside his coat. Savannah watched, as if entranced; it was like the beginning of a dance, this encounter between them, this first sweet, fiery union. She had expected to feel fear; instead, she felt excitement and anticipation. She'd been a girl when Burke entered her life and turned it upside down, but she was a woman now, and she wasn't afraid to trust her assessment of this man she'd married. She could believe in him.

Pres unbuttoned his cuffs, rolled his sleeves loosely, midway up his forearms. His manner was cool, but his eyes were hot as branding irons. Where Burke had been a mere boy, and a selfish one, at that, Pres was a man, in every sense of the word, and the very grace of his movements bespoke tenderness, power, and skill.

"You're sure?" he prompted quietly. "We can still go back and have Jacob tear up the papers, but once we've been—" he actually stumbled, just there, and reddened a little, "once we've been intimate, Mrs. Parrish, it's for life."

It was a gallant offer; he was giving her the chance to change her mind, with no apparent repercussions. She shook her head, began to unbutton the bodice of her dress.

He sat down on the edge of the mattress and, very gently, put her hands aside to take up the task himself. She trembled, sitting there, feeling every pass of his fingers, no matter how light, watching the subtle changes in his face as he unveiled her that first time. It was all so new, so fresh, so poignant.

Her breasts were bared; their tips tightened in response to the coolness of the air and, conversely, to the heat of Pres's gaze. He weighed her tenderly in the palms of his hands, chafed the already-taut nipples with the pads of his thumbs. "Lovely," he breathed. A slight, sleepy smile crooked his mouth at one corner and twinkled in his eyes. "Oh, Savannah, you do make me believe in good things again. A Grecian statue awash in moonlight couldn't be more beautiful than you are."

She was stricken with a sort of quiet joy; such words, coming from this man who was usually straightforward to the point of poor manners, were beyond precious. Tears prickled her eyes. "You've got poetry in you, Dr. Parrish," she whispered, and shivered with pleasure because he was still plying her, still preparing her for the inevitable conquest. "I would never have guessed."

The smile crooked again. "I'm full of surprises," he said, and then he bent his head and began kissing and nibbling his way down her neck, across the length of her collarbone and, finally, along the rounded swell of her upper breast. When he boldly took her nipple, she gasped; the sensation was like waltzing amid flames of pleasure.

Gently, he pressed her back onto the pillows, and somehow managed to divest her of most of her clothes while still feasting at first on one nipple, then the other. Savannah, stripped of all but her garters, stockings, and velvet slippers, moaned and arched her back.

"Ummm," Prost murmured. "Be patient, Mrs. Parrish. These things should take time."

"I don't want it to take time," Savannah gasped. "I want you now."

He chuckled. The windows were fogged, and the soft rain whispered over their heads. "So that's the way of it, is it? For shame." He moved down her rib cage to kiss a light circle around her navel; his breath radiated through her like sunlight on a hot day. She was perspiring when he finally sat up, and very short of breath. Everything inside her seemed knotted into a single straining ache. "Where is your patience? Where is your virtue?" he teased.

"To hell with my virtue," Savannah whimpered and, locking her hands behind his neck, she drew him down for her kiss. "To hell with yours, for that matter," she added, barely able to speak, when it was over.

The tide had turned, to her delight; she could see that Pres was losing control, that the kiss had robbed him of that damnable cool efficiency of his. He groaned, muttered an imprecation and got rid of his own clothes so quickly that some magician might have cast a spell to melt them away.

Savannah was still wearing her stockings and garters, though she had managed to kick off the slippers. Pres lay between her legs—he seemed bigger, heavier, and harder, now that he was naked—and drew up her knees with his hands, to make her more accessible.

"Savannah—?"

She laid an index finger to his lips. "Yes, Pres," she said, answering the incomplete question. "Oh, God, yes."

He hesitated only a moment, then arranged himself and entered her in one forceful thrust of his hips. Pleasure surged into her with him, interwoven with a brief, fierce pain, pleasure so intense that it forced out all other sensation, and Savannah cried out in jubilation and despair, surrender and challenge.

He withdrew, delved again, and the sensation was even keener that time, for both of them. His face was set for a grim and primitive struggle, as old as mankind, his powerful arms held the upper part of his body suspended above Savannah's breasts and belly, above her heart.

"Let go, Pres," she pleaded. "Please, please—let go—"

It was all unleashed then, all the loneliness, all the yearning, all the sorrow and pain that belonged to both of them. The joy came too, at long, long last, even more fierce than the storm of emotions that had cleared the way for it. They moved together with a force made of desperation, a holy, healing thing created out of both their minds, both their bodies, both their spirits.

Release overtook them simultaneously, and only after they had exhausted themselves to achieve it; Savannah was consumed by hers, calling out his name as a series of sharp tremors shook her, from the inside out. When she could breathe and see again, she looked up into Pres's face, watched as he moved in the last throes of his own climax.

Finally, he fell beside her, gasping, their bodies still joined. Savannah stroked his damp hair, let her fingers delve deep into it. "I love you," she said; the confession had simply escaped her, unplanned.

He lifted his head, searched her eyes. "You do?"

She waited a moment, her teeth buried in her lower lip, then nodded. No sense in denying it now. She'd told the truth, to herself and to him, but she wished she hadn't. Very possibly, she'd spoiled everything.

He kissed her lightly, tenderly, on the mouth. "I've never been in love before," he said, at long last. "Oh, there have been women, of course. Plenty of them. But nobody I cared about, until you. Even so, I feel something for you, Savannah, something deep, something that will last. Maybe it's love, I don't know. But whatever it is, it's good."

She blinked away tears, happy ones. "That's enough for now, isn't it?"

He chuckled and ran a lazy hand up her belly to cup her left breast and play with the peak. "I guess that depends on whether you're talking about the feeling, or all the things I want to do to you in and out of this bed."

Savannah slipped her arms around his neck. "Why, Doctor. I do believe you're something of a rascal."

"As far as you're concerned," he said, hardening within her, exciting her anew, seeking the same breast with his mouth, now that his hand had mapped the way, "I'm the devil. And this time, wife, we're taking it slowly. After all, we've got all night."

Soon, she was writhing and pleading and bucking beneath his fingers and his lips again, but he took her at his leisure, and he was a long, long time at it.

They were entwined, both of them deeply asleep, when, sometime in the depths of the night, a loud pounding sound awakened them.

"Doc!" Trey shouted, from the other side of the door. "Doc, wake up! Quick!" More hammering. "Damn it, wake up!"

"I'm on my way!" Pres yelled back, already out of bed and scrambling into his clothes, from the sounds of it, without benefit of a lamp. He'd probably had a lot of practice, Savannah concluded, in sleepy shock, getting dressed in the dark, rushing to answer some urgent summons. "Hold your horses!"

Savannah sat up, blinking, and moved across the mattress to reach for matches and fumble with the globe on the lantern. By that time, Pres was already in the front room, technically his office, opening the door. His tones were low, even, calming. Trey, for his part, sounded frantic. Although she strained to hear what was happening, she couldn't quite make out the words.

She arose—she was a doctor's wife now, after all, even if she'd only been one for a few hours—and hastily donned a practical calico dress. She was still wearing her garters and stockings, she noticed, with a slight blush, and quickly found her slippers, one on one side of the room, one on the other.

Pres had shrugged into his coat and grabbed his battered medical bag by the time Savannah joined him and Trey in the front room. "What is it?" she asked, thinking Rachel must be ill, or Emma. Trey's face was the color of dried clay.

"It's Jacob." Pres flung the words to her, over one shoulder, as he went out. "From the symptoms, it sounds as if his heart might be failing."

With that shattering news, he was gone, Trey following close behind him.

Savannah gripped the back of one of the packing-crate chairs, stunned. Jacob? He'd always seemed impervious, and though she'd only known him and June-bug for a short time, both of them meant a great deal to her. They were more than friends, they were family, almost like parents. She yanked her cloak down from its peg by the wall and dashed into the night after her husband.

She didn't call out to him to wait; she knew he couldn't match his pace to hers, and wouldn't, not in an emergency. He was a shadow up ahead, sprinting through the darkness toward the station, Trey right beside him. The Hargreaves' house, too, was spilling light from every shiny new window.

"No," Savannah prayed, in an anxious murmur, as she ran after the two men, noticing only when she slipped and nearly fell that it was still raining, that the ground was blanketed in mud. "Please, God. Don't take Jacob. June-bug needs him—we all need him—please—"

June-bug was up, of course, when Savannah burst into the station, silver-threaded brown hair trailing down her back. She looked like a young girl in her white flannel nightdress and wrapper, but every year of her life showed in her deep blue eyes. Seeing Savannah, she held out both arms, asking for comfort and, at the same time, offering it.

Savannah embraced her hard. "How is he?" she asked, a moment later.

"I don't know," June-bug said distractedly. She started to walk toward the back, where she and Jacob slept, then stopped and took a few steps in the direction of the stove.

"Sit down," Savannah said gently. "I'll make you some tea."

June-bug took a seat in one of the rocking chairs facing the hearth—the very place where Savannah and Pres had been married such a short time before—and stared blindly into the fire. "What would I do, without my Jacob?" she whispered.

Savannah was making the tea when she became aware of young Toby; he was crouched in the space between the stove and the pantry wall, his knees drawn up to his chest, his head down. He was the personification of despair, and when he looked up at Savannah, her heart turned over.

"He's strong," she said. It was all she had to offer at the moment, all he would accept from her, she expected. Otherwise, she might have taken him into her arms right then, like any frightened child in need of comforting.

Toby simply nodded and rested his head on his knees again.

Savannah brewed tea, poured it, brought a cup to June-bug, and a cup for herself. Neither of them touched the concoction; sometimes it was the ritual that was needed, rather than the tea itself, and that was one of those occasions.

The chair squeaked as June-bug rocked slowly back and forth, still gazing into the fire. "We was getting ready for bed," she said, lapsing deeper into the hill-country vernacular of her youth than usual, no doubt because of her distress. "Jacob jest put a hand to his chest and said, 'Why, June-bug, I don't believe I feel the way I ought.' That was all. He turned real white and laid down on the bed and shut his eyes to sleep, but I could see he was in terrible pain. Jest terrible. And it got worse and worse, until finally I woke up Toby and sent him to fetch Trey." She looked at Savannah, blinked quickly and swallowed. "I reckon I forgot we have a doctor at Springwater now, I was so wrought up."

Savannah reached across to pat June-bug's arm. "Do you want to go in and sit with him?"

"He told me I'd be in the way, that I should give the doc room enough to get close and take a look at him." June-bug's eyes were suddenly brilliant with tears, and she laid a hand to her bosom, fingers splayed, as though willing her heart to beat for Jacob, as well as for her. "I'll tell you what I think—I think Jacob don't want me lookin' on when he dies. Old fool. He's got a vain streak in him, you know, even if he does have a way with the Word of God."

Savannah wanted to weep along with her friend, but this wasn't the time. Pres was in the McCaffreys' room with Jacob, doing everything he could, and she had a great deal of confidence in his abilities as a physician. Everyone at Springwater did, for he'd proven himself, treating his cowboy patients and dealing amiably with crotchety old settlers like Granny Johnson. For now, Savannah thought it wiser to keep her own emotions in check, insofar as possible, and provide support for June-bug.

"If anybody can save him, Pres can," she said softly.

June-bug nodded. "Doc and the Lord. That's who

we've got to count on now. Doc and the Lord and Jacob himself, of course."

It seemed as if hours had passed before Pres finally came out of the sickroom, Trey still trailing him like a worried shadow, but it was probably not more than thirty minutes or so. He pulled his stethoscope from his neck and tossed it into his bag, and his eyes were bleak as his gaze strayed first to Savannah, as if seeking courage, then moved on to June-bug.

"He's alive," he said. "But it's bad. Even if he lasts the night and gets through the next few days, he's got a long road ahead of him."

Savannah wanted to go to her husband, put her arms around him, share her strength as he had shared his, but at this point it wouldn't be a favor. She stood beside June-bug's chair, with a hand on her friend's shoulder, and regarded him in silence.

Pres sighed and rubbed the back of his neck with one hand. "You'd best get some rest," he said to June-bug. "There's no point in exhausting yourself."

June-bug squared her shoulders and raised her chin. "Women have been sittin' up, keepin' vigils, for longer than God's Aunt Bessie can remember. I didn't get to watch over my boys before they was taken, but I will surely sit beside my husband and hold his hand."

A lump formed in Savannah's throat; she swallowed hard and reminded herself not to cry for Jacob, for June-bug, for their lost sons, and for the grieving families of all the other sons and brothers and fathers who would never come marching home, even though the war was long ended.

"I need to stay here for the rest of the night, Savannah," Pres said. "Trey will walk you back home."

She shook her head and spoke at last. "I'm not leaving," she said. "I'm a doctor's wife, remember?"

The shadow of a smile touched his mouth, that mouth that had wreaked such havoc with her senses only a few hours before, in their bed. She wanted Pres, suddenly, not in the passionate, playful way of the wedding night just past, but in a primal manner that had more to do with the affirmation of life itself. She knew he felt the same way, that when they were alone again, however long the interim might be, they would make love in a ferocious, elemental celebration of heartbeats and sunrises, wildflowers and the smells of baking bread and hot coffee, and a multitude of other blessings, small and large.

June-bug rose a little shakily from her chair; Savannah was ready to catch her if need be, but Jacob's wife was the most stalwart of women, despite her diminutive size, and she would not fall. "I've got to go to him," she said.

Savannah merely nodded.

"The children—they'll be frightened," June-bug fretted, raising a slightly tremulous hand to her mouth. "Poor little Toby, why he thinks the sun surely rises and sets in Jacob McCaffrey."

"I'll look after both of them," Savannah said quietly. "You just concentrate on Jacob and yourself."

June-bug nodded, and her eyes glittered with fresh tears. "Thank you," she said, and then she turned and went in to sit with her husband.

Pres's look held admiration. "Yes," he affirmed, to Savannah, before following June-bug into the corridor at the back. "Thank you."

Trey lingered, looking torn, as well as exhausted and worried.

"Go home, Trey," Savannah said. "Rachel and Emma are probably waiting for word, and there's nothing more you can do here."

"You'll send someone, if we're needed?"

"Yes," she promised. "I'll come myself."

That satisfied Trey, evidently, for he left, and after a few minutes, Savannah went to the window and saw the lights in the mail-order house go out one by one.

After a little interval spent gathering her thoughts, she turned and walked briskly over to the stove. The boy was still sitting where she'd last seen him, huddled against the wall, the picture of abject misery.

"Toby," she said firmly,

He looked up at her, blue eyes filled with injury and defiance. He would grow to be a handsome man, she thought, of the rakish variety. He did not speak.

"How old are you?"

"Eleven," he answered, after a long time. He was small for his age; no doubt that was one of the many reasons why he behaved like such a cocky little rooster when he felt threatened.

"Not so very old, then," she said. "Come out of there." She extended a hand and waited.

Amazingly, he took the offered hand and rose, mostly under his own power, but with a little tug from Savannah. In a very matter-of-fact way, she led the child to the hearth, sat down in June-bug's rocking chair, and took him onto her lap. He tried briefly to pull away, then sagged against her in relieved defeat, and she held him, careful to avoid making him feel restricted.

"You love Jacob very much, don't you?" she said, into his fair, straight hair.

He nodded, his head propped beneath her chin. She felt the wetness of tears through the bodice of her dress, but of course did not mention them.

"So do I. So does Dr. Parrish. He'll do everything he can to help Jacob get well, Toby. I can promise you that much, at least."

The boy snuffled, relaxed a little more. And after that, no more words were needed. Savannah simply rocked, and Toby nestled against her until, at last, he slept.

Jacob survived that night, and the days and nights to come, as well. By the time the leaves began to change colors, he was up and about, with the use of a cane. He could not do his former heavy work, and he was pale and gaunt; it seemed to Savannah and to everyone else at Springwater, that something vital had gone out of him. He rarely preached of a Sunday morning, or even spoke of the Lord, fondly or otherwise. He even left off working on the beautiful cradle he'd been crafting for the Hargreaves baby, Rachel's pregnancy being an acknowledged fact, now that Pres had properly examined her.

Savannah feared that Jacob was about the business of

dying; he was simply taking his time with it. It was plain that he'd given up the struggle.

She felt guilty for the wild, private happiness she and Pres had found together. They made love every chance they got, often enough that it didn't matter how inadequate their little rusted stove was because they didn't need it to keep them warm. Pres treated a lot of patients—they seemed to come from nowhere—in off the surrounding ranges, down out of the foothills, from passing wagon trains, from line shacks and farms and ranches, far and wide. Savannah helped him, learned to sterilize wounds and even stitch them closed, and how to set broken limbs, too. Mostly, though, she just kept the sick and injured distracted while Pres did whatever mending that happened to be needed.

Autumn was on the horizon, and still Jacob's spirits did not rise. Savannah knew Pres thought about the other man often, as she did as well, at a loss for how to help him. She didn't need to be told that her husband had seen such cases before, and that he was very troubled.

The women of the community made no effort to hide the fact that they were curious about Savannah, apparently wondering if she went around Springwater and her husband's office wearing feathers, face paint, and beads.

The last week of September brought a string of summery, blue-skied days. A celebration was planned, partly in the hope of raising Jacob's spirits. That Sunday, after Landry Kildare had delivered a layman's sermon, the men carried tables out of the station and set it in the withering grass under June-bug's carefully nurtured trees; food was produced and eaten. Tales of bitter cold winters were told, perhaps as a hex against the trials of the one to come, of sick children and animals, and suffering Indians passing through. Then the men went off to play a game of horseshoes.

Evangeline Wainwright, eyes sparkling, produced a sewing box from the back of the family wagon, and the others did the same. Savannah, having nothing to fetch, stayed behind, as unsure of herself as ever.

The food and dishes were cleared away, and then the mysterious boxes and bags were opened, to reveal quilt blocks in every imaginable shade—blue and yellow, green and red, purple and brown. All were carefully stitched into the wedding ring pattern.

"Are we agreed, ladies?" Evangeline asked, of the assembly.

Rachel, already big with the forthcoming baby, was the first to nod in accord. She too had produced quilt blocks, having sent Emma across the way to fetch them. The others looked at each other, faces full of silent questions, but then they all nodded, too, and even smiled. Within moments, the tabletop was covered in colorful pieces of fabric.

"The quilt is for you, Savannah," Evangeline said softly.

Savannah put a hand to her heart, overwhelmed. She had been wishing she had needlework to contribute, thinking that might make them more likely to accept her. "For me?" she echoed, sure there must be some mistake. "A stranger?"

"Most of us were strangers, one time or another," said Mrs. Bellweather. "Out here, we all need each other."

Rachel beamed, fairly bouncing with friendly excitement. "We said we'd piece a quilt for the next Springwater bride, remember? Back when the house was raised? You're that bride, Savannah."

Savannah blinked rapidly, but it didn't do any good. Tears spilled down her cheeks anyway, and she smiled through them, as brightly, June-bug would later say, as the sun shining through clouds. *She'd* been the one to erect barriers between herself and the others, she realized, just as Emma had once said. She had been so afraid of being rejected that she'd never given Rachel and the others a real chance.

"I don't know how to thank you," she whispered.

Evangeline laughed. "I'll tell you how," she said. "Sit down and help us finish this up. We'll plan a quilt for the *next* bride as we work."

It felt so very good, just to take a place among them, to belong, to be a part of their plans, privy to their secrets, their hopes, their dreams and sorrows. She fit in nicely between Rachel and Sue Bellweather.

"I say we do a crazy quilt this time," Sue said. "We'll just put the pieces together any old which way and see what happens."

There was a brief conference, and everyone agreed. A crazy quilt it would be.

Savannah dried her cheeks with the back of one hand, trying to be subtle about it, and reached for a square of bright pink and white gingham. Never having participated in a quilting bee before, she was relieved that there wouldn't be a complicated pattern to follow.

Evangeline was looking down the length of the table at Miranda, who carried her baby boy in a sling, close against her bosom, head down, snipping shyly at a piece of worn green velvet, shaping it into a triangle.

"Maybe you'll be the next bride, Miranda," Evangeline said gently.

"None too soon, either," remarked Sue Bellweather, only half under her breath.

"Oh, hush yourself," June-bug scolded. She was subdued, because of Jacob's illness, but she was enjoying her friends' company all the same. "Everything in this world happens when it ought to, and that's a fact."

Savannah thought of the wedding ring quilt that would soon grace the bed she and Pres shared, and felt a rush of joy so sweet and poignant that it hurt her heart. Then she took in the dear faces around that table, awash in firelight, and rejoiced that, at long, long last, she was home.

Linda Lael Miller

SPRINGWATER SEASONS

Rachel

Savannah

Miranda

Jessica

The breathtaking new series....Discover the passion, the pride, and the glory of a magnificent frontier town!

Coming soon from Pocket Books

2043

LINDA LAEL MILLER

TWO BROTHERS

THE GUNSLINGER

THE LAWMAN

"Linda Lael Miller's talent knows no
bounds...each story she creates is...superb."
—*Rendezvous*

**Available now
from Pocket Books**

2009-01